Awards for *Nowhere Ranch*

Winner, 2011 Rainbow Awards,
1st Place Contemporary Erotica

Nominee, 2011 Cupid & Psyche Awards, BDSM

Best Book of 2011, GLBT-BDSM,
The Romance Reviews

This book is a work of fiction. The names, characters, places and incidents are products of the writer's imagination or have been used fictitiously and are not to be construed as real. Any resemblance to persons, living or dead, actual events, locale or organizations is entirely coincidental.

Heidi Cullinan, POB 425, Ames Iowa 50010

Nowhere Ranch
Copyright © 2015 by Heidi Cullinan
ISBN: 978-0-9961203-1-9
Print Edition
Edited by Sasha Knight
Cover by Kanaxa

All Rights Are Reserved. No part of this book may be used or reproduced in any manner whatsoever without written permission, except in the case of brief quotations embodied in critical articles and reviews.

First publication 2011
First Heidi Cullinan publication 2015
www.heidicullinan.com

Love will grow through the cracks you leave open.

Ranch hand Roe Davis absolutely never mixes business with pleasure—until he runs into his boss, Travis Loving, at the only gay bar within two hundred miles.

Getting involved with the ranch owner is a bad idea, but Roe's and Travis's bedroom kinks line up against one another like a pair of custom-cut rails. As long as they're both clear this is sex on the side, no relationship, no interfering with the job, they could make it work.

Shut out by his family years ago, Roe survived by steadfastly refusing to settle into so much as a post office box. As his affair with Travis grows into more than just sex, Roe's past catches up with him, threatening the thin ray of happiness he's found, reminding him it's well past time he went on his way.

But even a loner gets lonely, and at this point, there's nowhere left to run. The shame and sorrow of what he's lost will stay with Roe wherever he goes— until he's ready to let love lead him home.

Praise for Heidi Cullinan

"Heidi Cullinan is one of the undisputed queens of scorching gay romance. Long may she reign!"

—Christopher Rice,
New York Times Bestselling Author

"Cullinan…blends appreciation for down-home values with hopes for gay equality"

—Publisher's Weekly

"…political and powerful and brilliant"

—Dear Author

Five enthusiastic stars!

—The Romance Reviews

"Heidi knows how to make well rounded characters that feel *real*."

—My Fiction Nook

"There's something magical within the pages of these books."

—Rainbow Book Reviews

"If the heart is akin to a musical instrument, Ms. Cullinan played it beautifully."

—Mrs. Condit & Friends Read Books

"…real, raw sex combined with an emotional connection"

—Fiction Vixen

Nowhere Ranch

Heidi Cullinan

for Jan

Acknowledgments

Many thanks to Marie Sexton, Signy Kuiper, Sue Danic, Libby Drew, Dan Cullinan, and Jason for beta reading, to Jules Robin for editing the first edition. Thanks to Saritza Hernandez for being a five-star agent and Sasha Knight for being my favorite editor on planet Earth.

1

MY NAME IS Monroe Davis, and this is the story of how I found home.

Once, home was Algona, Iowa. Growing up, everybody couldn't wait to leave it, but I could have stayed forever. I still miss it sometimes. I miss the way the trees are thick and leafy, and the way the fields of corn and soybeans ripple in the wind as you drive through the countryside. I miss the way the earth bakes in August, moist and rich and full of life. I miss going to potlucks in the church basement, miss the annual Fourth of July parade full of people I've known since birth. But there came a point where I had to leave, because it wasn't home, not anymore.

It started when my mom found my porn. She was cleaning my room, and for whatever reason she decided to clean out my bedside drawer too, all the way to the bottom, and she stumbled onto my stash. She gave it to my dad, who came straight out to me in the field. When I saw him coming, I turned off the tractor and ran to meet him because I thought something had happened, that someone had been hurt.

But he didn't say anything. He just held up those magazines and DVDs and looked at me, waiting for me to explain. Except it was exactly what he'd already figured out, so I lowered my head and stared at the alfalfa under my boots as my breathing got funny. The blood rushed around in my head, and sweat ran down my neck.

After a long, painful silence, Dad turned around and headed to the house.

I got on the tractor and finished raking the hay because I didn't know what else to do.

They sent the pastor of our church to talk to me. He told me about hell and how *my lifestyle* would send me there. He explained how my choices were an abomination to God and an insult to the good name of my family. My dad wouldn't look me in the eye, and my mom cried all the time. My brother, Bill, acted like I'd punched him in the gut.

You would have thought I'd murdered somebody's baby. I guess to them, I did. Except I was the same Roe they'd always known. They just hadn't known about the part I'd kept quiet.

Bill was the first to finally talk to me. He said after praying, and with Pastor's help, the family came to a decision. It would be okay if I stayed, but I needed to get counseling from Pastor Tim. Bill also told me about some nice girls I should think about dating. He hinted he knew a few who would be okay for just sex, though I couldn't tell Mom about that. But I had to do the counseling, and there could be no more gay porn and no more gay, period. It was either this or leave the farm.

Well, I left.

I didn't leave town, though, and mostly I ran around getting into trouble. It took me little more than half a year to end up in prison because of a really bad bar fight. This was after lots of times in lockup and a half a dozen random charges, all about drinking and fighting. They gave me three years, which turned into one, and then they let me out at eight months because of overcrowding. I wore my ankle bracelet, kept my head down and was good to my probation officer.

When they turned me loose for good, I got out of Algona.

I was tired of it. Tired of letting other people make me feel like shit. Tired of people treating me as if I had the plague. Tired of alternating between blaming everybody else for my problems and thinking if I acted guilty enough they might forgive me.

I got tired of waiting for home to come to me. So I made damn sure I never needed home again.

As you can imagine, life eventually got the better of me.

I MET TRAVIS Loving when I went to work at Nowhere Ranch. I'd been shuffling around ranches throughout the Midwest, doing time in Kansas and the Dakotas.

Nowhere, in northwestern Nebraska, was the farthest west I'd yet gone. I will admit I answered the ad because of the name. Also because if I went through one more fucking North Dakota winter, I was going to hang myself. I'd heard it wasn't quite as bad in Nebraska. So after a few good days of partying in Omaha, I contacted the ranch manager, who said he'd give me a try, and off I went.

The other thing I liked about Nowhere Ranch was it was a hobby ranch, almost as small as a larger farm. I know everybody's all about the sexy Southern cowboys and big ranches and tumbleweeds blowing by you, but I grew up on a farm, and it's what I know. Ranches usually feel too big. It's the wrong culture or something.

Nowhere Ranch was smaller, and it was way out in the boondocks—hence, the name. Apparently when Loving bought it, he kept talking about how he was moving out to the middle of nowhere, and the name stuck. It was a good, solid operation, especially considering the owner was still pretty green. The feed was all organic, and he had about as many sheep as he did cattle. We only had sheep a short while at Dad's farm, but I knew enough about them to understand what I was getting into.

None of the other hands lived on site, which worried me at first. But the manager said it really was a small operation, and they rotated through a set of local guys when they needed them. He also said if I wasn't fussy, there was an apartment above the stable I was welcome to. It wouldn't cost me anything if I was willing to be on standby to do work off the clock, like help round up steers that got out. So it would only be me and the owner at the ranch, with the manager and his family down the road.

As soon as I heard about having my own apartment, not a bunk with other guys, I was ready to do about anything to get there. I was careful about anybody finding out I was queer, but I still couldn't shake the feeling something I didn't expect would trip me up. I was pretty sure handling sheep and calves wasn't going to give me away, but in my own place I could jerk off without watching to make sure nobody noticed there was nothing but dick in the mags and vids I had.

Except the apartment was a real fucking dive. It was about twelve by twelve, and I think the carpet had been there since 1972 without once making the acquaintance of a vacuum. It was furnished, with a bed and a table and a recliner and a nightstand, but I took one look at the bedding and headed to Walmart to replace it. While I was there I picked up a bottle of bleach too. But I was still overall pleased with the place. After a little cleaning and replacement parts, it was a palace to me.

The only problem was there really wasn't a kitchen to speak of, just a dorm-sized fridge and a hot plate. I'm not any kind of fancy chef, but eating out all the time is expensive, and I get tired of sandwiches. It was enough of a hitch in my get-along that I thought about asking for a proper stove, but in the end I decided I could limp along to start. I'd lobby for a moderate kitchen upgrade once I had a better lay of the land. If I even stayed long enough to bother with it.

The first two weeks I only saw Loving in passing, usually in the mornings as he stood with the manager, Tory Parrish, at the fence rail. Tory would nod while Loving spoke quietly, his tan cowboy hat bobbing as he turned this way and that, gesturing to fields and barns and equipment. Occasionally I also saw Loving head out on his horse a couple hours after the last of the hands had gone home and he'd had his evening meeting with Tory. Sometimes I would watch him ride out, because it was a nice vista, man on horse, silhouetted against the sunset.

Loving was tall and broad, a few inches shorter than my six-two. Handsome in a way I appreciated, but he was significantly older than me. By this time I was almost twenty-five, and Loving had to be pushing forty. He seemed more like my dad than somebody to ogle. Also, he's the boss. I knew he used to be a professor in Omaha and he was divorced with no kids, and I knew he'd only owned this ranch for about three years. Mostly I didn't pay him much attention outside of noting when he was around so I could work harder at not being a dick. Because I did like the job, and outside of the mediocre kitchen, I enjoyed the apartment.

One Saturday night there was a knock on my door, and when I opened it, by God if it wasn't Loving standing there. He gave me a curt nod as a greeting.

"We got trouble on the north ridge. Can I get you to lend a hand?"

I said sure. After hustling into my boots, I grabbed my hat and followed him down the stairs.

Tory was already on a four-wheeler, rifle stowed in the back. Loving had his own ride waiting beside Tory's, but I noticed there wasn't a third, so I climbed on behind Tory and held on to the rack as we rode.

When I saw the ewe bobbing around in the field, bumping into the other sheep and acting like she was drunk, I knew what we were in for.

"It looks neurological." Loving sounded uncertain though, and Tory shrugged.

"It's neurological all right," I said. "That ewe has rabies."

They both turned to me, surprised. "How can you tell?" Tory asked.

I motioned to the ewe. "She's acting all crazed. It's eating her brain right now. We've got to put her down and get her the hell out of here. Need to isolate the rest of this herd right quick. Groups as small as you can get. You don't know how many she's bit."

"I'll call the vet." Loving reached for his phone.

I shook my head. "Ain't no point."

"But there's a treatment," Loving pressed. "They give it to people."

"Yeah. And it's several thousand dollars a pop. This is thirty head of sheep. You'd do better to slaughter them and get new." I gestured to the huddled herd.

"Partition them off as best you can and wait it out, is my advice. Either they been infected or not. All you can do is wait and see." I tugged on the brim of my hat. "What you *do* need to do is call all the hands and make sure none of them's been bit. You only got so many hours between exposure and death."

Loving reached for his phone again, but Tory already had his out and waved him off.

"I'll call the boys. You two get her put down and figure out how the fuck we're going to isolate them."

Loving grabbed the rifle, nodding at me as he loaded the cartridges. "You're sure about this?"

Hell yes, I was sure. "They get it from skunks, see. Anyway, it's the sort of thing you don't mess around with. She could infect half the herd tonight. Better to kill her and find out I'm wrong than wait and lose them all. The only positive test is to examine her brain. Which kind of requires her to be dead."

Loving grimaced and nudged his hat higher on his head with his knuckle. "And here I thought foot rot was hell."

"Oh, everything about sheep is hell. We never cussed more than the years we raised them."

Loving sighed and raised the rifle, only to lower it again. "Would you mind trying to separate her a little? But don't expose yourself."

Heading for the main body of the herd, I clapped my hands and called, "*Hee-yah*," until they started to bleat and stumble over each other trying to get away.

The rabid ewe followed them for a second before she fell. She got up pretty quickly, and when she did, she came for me.

Sheep don't exactly set land-speed records, but I hustled out of the way because I wasn't interested in catching any stray gunshot. Turns out I needn't have worried, as Loving could shoot a single hair off your head at half a mile. He put the bullet right between her eyes, and she went down like a ton of bricks.

Tory tucked his phone back into his pocket. "I got hold of everybody. All the boys are coming in to help sort them out. I thought probably in the stalls in the horse barn. Chaucer and the boys won't hurt to be out in the pasture a few days, and we can whip up temporary pens in the south field."

That's what we did. We ended up only losing two more sheep total, which was good. But I didn't talk to Loving for the rest of the week. On Friday, he took off. Tory said he'd be gone through the weekend.

I thought maybe this would be a good time to get away myself. I was starting to get itchy. I headed into town to the public library, where an online search for nearby gay bars informed me I would be going three hours north to Rapid City to get laid. I know they have them fancy apps on smartphones to hook up, but I can't abide putting that kind of money down for a piece of plastic.

I worried Tory would say I couldn't leave the ranch unattended, but he said not to bother about it, as he always kept an eye out when Loving was gone. He said I was to go on and have a nice time.

The drive was okay. Mostly I didn't notice anything around me, too busy thinking about how I could spend the next forty-eight hours fucking and getting fucked. I checked into my hotel, showered, and fussed with my clothes before heading over at nine.

The bar was small and sad, nothing like the flashy stuff I'd gotten used to in Omaha and Kansas City. In North Dakota I had gone to Fargo, which hadn't been bad. This place was a different story. There was hardly anybody there, and most of them had already hooked up. But I saw one lone cowboy sitting at the bar, and I bee-lined to him, determined to spread my legs even if he looked like Ethel Merman.

You probably saw this coming, but I have to tell you, you could have knocked me over with a feather when the cowboy turned around and he was Travis Loving.

2

FOR A SECOND we gaped at each other, and yeah, I was flipping out. I mean, the one guy at a ranch you work *really* hard to make sure doesn't find out you're gay is the fucking boss. So I stood there and tried not to piss myself. Then it occurred to me there was only one reason he would be there, same as me.

He touched the tip of his hat, nodding at the stool beside him. "Buy you a drink?"

I sat down, still dazed. The bartender asked for my order twice before I could stutter I'd take a beer, please. He gave me a draw, and I clung to the glass once it was in front of me, staring at it so I didn't have to look at Loving. Loving, who was queer.

"So," Loving said at last.

"Yeah," I agreed, and drank my beer.

We sat in heavily awkward silence for a few minutes.

"Usually busier in here." Loving swiped a gulp from his Michelob bottle. "Hell of a drive for a drink."

I gave a sort of nervous laugh and took off my hat

to rub at my hair, which was getting sweaty. "Three hours is quite a trip." I bit off *for a fuck* at the last second.

"Well, there is the Internet."

I snorted into my glass. "Yeah, I tried that. Once."

When Loving offered me a second round, I insisted it was my turn, and I bought his next Michelob. We sat there hunched over our stools without saying a word.

People had started coming in, but hooking up was not on my radar now. A few guys caught my eye, but I didn't know what Loving would make of my favorite kind of fuck. I'm not exactly leather, but I never say no if somebody from that scene looks my way.

To be honest, I kind of like the guys who make it clear they're there for your ass, end of discussion. When I was fourteen and seriously wanting to be fucked, I used to pray to God to send me aliens to fuck me and then leave. Anal probe: bring it on. Just don't park your boots by my bed. Once I hooked up with a guy who kept me all weekend at his house, but I swear we only said about twenty words to each other the whole time.

I worried what Loving would think of how my preferences ran, and he might find them out because sometimes the game began in the bar. I have a fondness for getting felt up in a booth, trying to look as if I'm not. I'm also not averse to ignoring those signs on the bathroom door and bending over the toilet, bracing my hands on the wall while I get it from behind.

Obviously I wasn't going to do that when my boss

could walk in to drain the hose.

I wanted to be somebody's slut for the night, to stop standing straight and impressing everybody. Instead I'd driven three hours to feel like I was still at work.

"I wish," Loving said after a half hour of more silence, "you could go up to them and say what you wanted. Better yet, we should have little cards to hand each other, listing preferences and pet peeves. God-damn, but I hate driving all this way only to find out I'm taking home a cross between a parrot and a squealing piglet."

That made me snort my beer. Loving passed me a napkin, deadpan, but there was a light in his eye that eased me.

"I've had guys come up and tell me what they want." I found it hot when they did.

Loving grunted. "When you're forty-two, that tactic doesn't work as well. I have a hard enough time picking out the ones who won't call me Grandpa when they brush me off."

"What are you after? Maybe I can help you weed through."

It was, I realized, a fucking forward thing to offer, and I retreated into my beer. But he seemed unfazed, only leaning on the bar and contemplating for another few minutes.

"Age isn't so much of an issue, but the space be-tween Tired Old Horse and Flighty Young Colt does seem to work out best." He sipped at his beer. "I really don't care much for talking. I don't want to know their history outside of whether or not we need to double the condom, and I don't want to give my story either. Tonight, they need to be somebody willing to take a rough ride." He glanced at me, rueful. "See any of those out there?"

Yeah. You're sitting next to him.

I took a long drink and wiped my mouth with the back of my hand. "Nope."

"I see plenty I think have my same agenda too. I don't stand a chance." Loving sighed. "What about you, Davis? What's on your menu?"

Oh, fuck. I searched desperately for something to say, but nothing would land in my head. I drained my beer and hoped he would get distracted and give up.

No dice.

"Shy boy, are you?" he teased.

"Around my boss, I am," I said, adding a silent prayer this conversation would end now.

"Here now." Loving turned on his stool to frown at me, his fingers tightening on his bottle of beer. "You think I'm going to hold this against you? Fire you to keep you quiet or something?"

Well, yeah, it had crossed my mind, though clearly he was offended by the idea. "To be honest, sir, I don't know what to think."

"I'll tell you what you're gonna think. That I'm not some dickhead who'll fire you to protect my secrets.

Which I don't have. I'm out, but I don't advertise." He tipped his hat back, and when the bartender brought me my beer, Loving held out a twenty before I could reach for my wallet. "I'm not your fucking boss tonight."

I took hold of the glass and anchored myself against it. "But you will be on Monday."

He grunted and smiled wryly. "Tell me what the fuck you're after, Davis. I told you my list. Let's hear yours."

I didn't have enough focused brain cells left to make up a lie, so I gave him the truth. "Let's just say there's *one* guy here who fits your bill. But he doesn't go to bed with the boss."

I kept my eyes on my beer, but I watched him out of the corner of my eye. He was still for a second, then motioned to the bartender for another drink. It wasn't until I was half through my beer I realized he had switched to soda.

"Tory says you're from Iowa."

I nodded. "Algona. It's a small town in the north-west-central area."

"I'm from Kansas City originally," Loving offered. "Married and moved to Omaha."

"Heard some of the hands say you were a professor."

"Mathematics. But shortly after my divorce, they cut my position." He grimaced. "Once I came out, it turns out they didn't need as many math professors. So I cashed in my savings and bought Nowhere."

I didn't know what to say. This was an awful lot of chatting for two guys who had said they didn't want any.

Of course, it was that or think about how we could be fucking each other.

I cleared my throat. "It's a nice spread."

Loving shrugged. "We had a rough go when we got started, but it's coming along. Thanks for picking up on the rabies so fast."

"It's why you hired me."

We ran out of conversation again, but I didn't get up, and even when a few guys were cruising me, I kept my head down. No matter what Loving said, it was weird to do a pick-up around him. Especially when I'd admitted if circumstances were different, *he* could have picked me up.

There was an easiness about him I really liked. We'd said next to nothing all night long, and yeah, it was awkward, but now that he'd established I wasn't going to get fired, I was starting to relax. I still wanted to get fucked, but this wasn't bad either. I told myself I'd go find a bed partner as soon as Loving got up to get his. In the meantime, I kept drinking, knowing I'd had too much, but Loving kept putting them in front of me.

Eventually I had to piss, though, so I excused myself and headed to the john. I figured by the time I got back, somebody else would have my seat, so I tipped my hat to Loving as I left and gave him a little smile too. I made a mental note of prospects on the way to the toilet, trying not to be disappointed in my options. I pissed and came out ready to go on the hunt.

Loving had left the bar and now sat in a booth in the back with two drinks in front of him. When he saw me, he motioned me over.

"They're starting music in a few minutes," he said. "We can see better from here."

I didn't want to sit and watch musicians. I wanted to find somebody to fuck me. But I couldn't say that, so I nodded, got my beer and headed for the other side of the booth.

He shook his head. "No. You won't be able to see from there." Scooting down, he indicated the space beside him. "Sit here."

As soon as the music started, his knee kept bumping mine, and after a few minutes his arm was behind me on the booth. It made me nervous, so I leaned forward to keep away from accidental touches. Except when he put his hand on my lower back, I knew it wasn't accidental.

When his fingers brushed against the patch of skin above my underwear, I jumped. But when his other hand landed on my thigh, I went still.

"This has nothing to do with your job," he whispered into my ear. "If you aren't interested because of me, say so now. But if your only objection is that I'm your boss—" He sighed. "Well, I'm going to make you say it a few more times, and I'm going to try and convince you otherwise." His hand gripped my thigh. "Think of it as a trial run. If we both like how it works out, we could save ourselves a lot of gas mileage."

My head was spinning. I held on to the table. "I don't know."

"If I weren't your boss," Loving dogged, "would I be barking up the right tree?"

His fingers were burning my skin, and I thought my jeans were on fire under his hand.

"Yes." I closed my eyes as he flirted with the elastic of my waistband.

"Good." I felt his fingertips against the patch of skin above my crack. "This bother you, being groped in public, or does it turn you on?"

"Second one."

His hands ran up and down my skin, setting off an erotic symphony inside me. "I was serious about wanting it rough. You all right with the occasional swat on your backside?"

Jesus. "That's fine."

He was stroking me openly now. Normally I wear a belt with my pants because they tend to slip down my ass, but I don't when I'm cruising because of the hopes someone will do exactly what Loving was doing, which was cupping his palm over the globe of my butt. His other hand fondled my cock through my jeans. "Anything specific you want me to do, or avoid?"

I bit my lip as his pinky finger dipped into my crack. I wanted this, but it was freaking me out. I had never, ever fucked anyone I knew before, let alone someone who employed me. I knew I should force the issue, should tell him no. But it was as if I were paralyzed.

His hands stilled. "You need to take a pass on my offer?" he asked. Gently. Almost kindly.

I opened my mouth to say yes, but I couldn't. *Jesus, what a headcase.* Taking a deep breath, I went for fucking broke. "I like rough." My voice got stronger as I went on. "I like it when I'm told what to do. If you want me ass up on the bed, you say so. Trash talking is good. You want to tell me I'm your pony or your dog you're fucking, that's okay. I think hotel carpets are gross, so I'd rather not do puppy play on the floor. But in bed's okay. You can tie me up or gag me, but I don't care for both at once. I don't do shower blowjobs because it makes me feel as if I'm drowning. I have done watersports, but I don't mind skipping that. Slapping is fine. So is biting as long as you don't draw blood. Pinching is good. Especially my nipples and my ass. Hickeys are okay, but I prefer to keep them where I can hide them."

I had started talking really fast by the end, and when I finished, I let out a breath and waited. After a few seconds, Loving's hand cupped my cock. "Public exposure?"

His fingers were already on my zipper. I shuddered and pushed my hips forward into his grip. "As long as I don't get arrested."

"Fair enough." He pinched my ass hard enough to make me jump. "Unbutton your fly and put your hands on the table."

3

Now that I'd made the decision to give in to Loving, I didn't see any reason not to sin big. I mean, if you're gonna steal a chicken, eat the whole damn thing.

I still had a bit of panic, but it was sliding quickly under my lust. Loving's fingers shifted against my ass as I fumbled with my fly. I undid all the buttons, but I was slow because he was kneading me hard from the back. I mean, *hard*. If he'd been a stranger, I'd have had him dial it down. But with Loving I felt okay with it. I finished with my jeans and put my hands on the table as he'd told me to do.

He pinched rough enough I felt it in my cock. "Good boy."

His hand on my thigh slipped up to my underwear. He stuffed his hand inside my briefs, taking my cock in a tight grip. I looked down and shivered at the sight of his hand moving beneath the fabric.

"You like watching me grab you right here where

anyone can see?"

"Yes, sir." I kept my eyes on the sight. I could see his hairy wrist at the waistband, the rest of his hand lost to its digging. I arched into his palm, humping a little.

He buried his finger into my crack, insistent this time. It pressed against my asshole, and I pushed back to let it in.

His fingertip only nudged gently at my hole. "We're doing this dry."

"Yeah. I can take it."

I listened carefully for his response. Some guys get off knowing I will do dry. Loving was hard to read, though. He said nothing, just pressed on in.

A dry finger up my ass is oddly focusing. It's sexy, and it's not. It's an invasion in a way lube isn't. It feels more like using to me, and to be done out in the open really turned me on. He had his finger up inside my ass all the way to the hilt while I watched his other hand moving roughly inside my pants, and holy shit, but I was ready to bend over the table here and now.

"I think it's time to move this to a private room," Loving said, but his hands were still working pretty insistently on and in me. "Your hotel or mine?"

"Yours." I liked the idea of being able to get away and end it, not having to wait until he decided. Of course, I couldn't drive because I was so drunk, so I wasn't going to have a car.

He played with me a little more, and so I started humping him, pushing into his hand. I could see other guys watching us out of the corner of my eye. I felt like such a whore. So cheap. Nasty and raunchy. I almost wished he could take me right here.

I moved faster on his finger.

He hooked it inside me, making me go still. He flexed his finger a few times, stroking my insides.

"You're nice and tight," he told me. "Clench around my finger." I did, but then his hand came out of my underwear and slid up inside my T-shirt. He pinched my nipple, crooked his finger again. "Harder. Work harder."

I milked him with my ass, and he rewarded me with several pinches on my nipples, first the left side and then the right. Pretty soon we had an audience, and I was gasping and rolling my hips. My hands had not left the table.

"They're going to kick us out," Loving remarked, but he didn't stop molesting me. He was tugging outright on my nipples now, pulling them sharply and then rolling them inside his fingers. "You like this, what I'm doing to you? Pinching you and fucking your ass?"

"I do."

"Is it too hard?"

I shook my head. "You can go a lot harder."

He pinched so hard I shuddered.

"They're watching you. Six guys at the tables in front of us. They know what I'm doing to you."

"Yeah." God, I was loving it.

"You truly are incredibly tight. Tell me how it feels to have my finger inside you."

"Hot." I clenched around him. "Hot and dirty."

"I want to watch my finger go in, with your hands holding your ass open while I push my finger inside you."

"Yes, sir," I said, wishing we were doing it already.

"Do you enjoy this, Monroe? Being fucked like this?"

"Yes, sir." But I had to add, "Please call me Roe, sir. Not even my mom called me Monroe."

"You're very polite. Are you calling me sir because I'm your boss, or because my finger is in your ass?"

"Both, sir."

He laughed, and to my disappointment, both his hands disappeared. But he pinched my ass before he withdrew completely. "Stand and do yourself up. We're going to go."

I did as I was told. I spared a glance at the men watching me. I'm only a little bit of an exhibitionist, but I liked knowing they'd seen. If they ever saw me again, they'd look at me and know I was a slut.

All the bad things everybody had said about me back home were true. I was degenerate and fit only for hell. Because if this was hell, then fucking sign me up.

The only thing I didn't care for was thinking that come Monday, no matter what else happened, Loving was going to know all about me too.

HIS HOTEL WAS the same as mine, a modest one on the edge of town. Unlike me, though, he had a king-size bed.

We didn't use it right away. He flipped on all the lights and cranked the AC because it was hot, and then he sat in the chair by the table and ordered me to take off my clothes. He watched as I did it, impassive and almost disinterested, which really turned me on. When I was naked, he had me stand there for a minute in front of him, turn around and bend over for an inspection.

"Very nice. Now come straddle my lap facing me and put your hands on top of your head."

He was a lot kinkier than I would have guessed, and I realized he was trying to see how far he could go. So I did my best to show he wasn't even close to the edge with me.

I sat still as he tugged on my nipples again, then played with my cock. But he was fixated on my chest. He flicked me awhile, and then, looking up at me, he leaned forward and bit one nipple lightly.

I swallowed against the pain. "Thank you, sir."

My cock hummed at the way he grinned. He slid to the other nipple and bit down even harder. This time I did cry out, and I thanked him again. We played this game for several minutes, until he gripped my thighs, lifted me to my knees and reached around to my ass. He slapped it sharply. "Open yourself."

I gasped as he pushed his finger—dry again—back inside me. "Thank you very much, sir," I said, when I was able.

"Thank you for what?" he prompted.

"For putting your finger in my ass." I bore down on him to take him farther inside of me.

"Tell me how my finger feels in your ass."

I began to pump on him a little. "Rough, sir. Your finger in my ass feels rough. It makes my stomach feel tight." A spark of instinct made me add, "It makes me feel ashamed."

Bingo. His finger pushed deeper. "Why ashamed?"

"Because your finger is fucking me." I fucked myself on it. "Because it's dry and rough, and you're fucking me, and I'm letting you. It's invading me, and I'm moaning for you like a slut."

His tongue stole out and wet a nipple. "You're polite enough on the ranch, but you're assertive too. Not here. You would do anything I told you right now, wouldn't you, Roe?"

"Yes, sir." It was true. I would.

"Even dirty things."

"Even dirty things, sir. Probably especially those."

He shut his eyes and sucked on my nipple as his finger fucked me. When he lifted his mouth, for a moment he fell out of character and looked up at me, questioning. "Is this how you always are in bed? Because I never would have suspected."

I fell out of my role too, but I kept after his finger with my ass. "I'm really in a mood for it tonight. You seem as if you are too."

His smile made my stomach dance. "Just as long—" He stopped, but oh yeah, I knew what he meant. So I helped him out.

"As long as I get this isn't all you are?" I grinned, feeling easy for the first time. "Yeah. I get it. And same to you."

A new pressure at my crack. "Can you take two? I don't want to hurt you, but this is very sexy."

"Try it," I suggested.

His finger pushed, but he looked uncertain. "Do you have a…word?"

I gave him a crooked smile. "To be honest, I really like *no*."

He laughed. When his fingers started to move, his face darkened. He slapped my ass cheek. "Hold yourself open more."

"Yes, sir." I complied.

The second finger was more a burn than actual pain. What I really loved was the way Loving's eyes smoldered as he watched me struggle. The way I would cry out, but he would push harder like my cries didn't matter. I don't know why it's so hot, and to be honest, it isn't always. But that night, with him, it was mother's milk. He took his time, ignoring my huffs and whines and cries, and then he was in to the hilt, two fingers raw and deep in me, wiggling, my hands holding my cheeks wide so he didn't have to work hard to get in there.

His free hand pinched my thigh. "What do you say?"

"Thank you, sir."

Another pinch. "What for?"

"Thank you, sir, for sticking two fingers raw up my ass."

"That's a good boy."

He leaned forward and took a nipple in his mouth, and his free hand came up to pinch the other one. He bit and pinched pretty hard, and I bucked against the pain, anchored from falling over only by his fingers buried inside my ass. His tongue circled around and around the nub, only to dart back as he took it in his teeth. He sucked. He tugged. He nipped. All the while he pushed into me, fucking me now with those two fingers. I felt him drawing back from me, not his body but his attention.

He was using me. He was sucking and fucking me, and he was lost in it. I moaned. I was so hard, so hot for him. Who cared that he was my boss. Who the fuck cared.

All at once he withdrew. "On the bed. Face down, ass up, knees wide. Hold still and don't say anything."

I did as I was told. He took a long time, but I remained obedient. Except eventually I realized I was playing the wrong game, so I twitched my ass at him, flexing my hole.

Bingo again.

He slapped my ass sharply, as if I'd gone into the cookie jar when I shouldn't. "I said wait. Hold still."

"Yes, sir."

Another slap.

"I said not to talk."

"I'm sorry, sir." I flexed my hole once more.

I have been with some spankers, but Loving is kind of his own thing when it comes to spanking. He got in some good slaps, and some of them made me quiver, but mostly he used this as an excuse to play with my ass. He slapped it, then slapped it a different way. I could tell he liked the sound of his hand on my flesh. Me too. When he got bored of spanking, he kneaded instead, pulling me wide open, grinding my cheeks open and shut, shifting them this way and that.

He pinched me again. God, the marks I was going to have.

At some point he'd grabbed lube because all of a sudden I felt wet and slick at my ass. It was two fingers into me, fast and deep, and my hungry ass took them in so well he didn't hesitate about adding a third. I was still tight, but I knew how to open. I felt him flirting with a fourth digit, which I wasn't sure I could do, not tonight.

He didn't press the issue, but he didn't let it drop entirely, either. "Have you let anybody fist you?"

"Yes."

His fingers flexed. "Did you enjoy it?"

I squirmed for him, grinding against his hand. "Kind of." The truth was, I'd been high, and I barely remembered except I had hurt like fuck the next day.

"I haven't done it. But I've read about how to do it. A lot." He shifted his fingers inside me. "I would love to do it to you sometime."

Sometime. Implying we would be doing this again. I

still wasn't sure about it, but I didn't want to wreck the moment, so I kept quiet and waited.

But he wanted more. "Do you want to feel my fist inside you?"

"Yes," I said, because, yeah, I would.

He began to thrust more regularly, making me open and sloppy with lube. "Your ass would swallow my hand. You would feel it deep inside you."

"I'd be so hot for your fist," I promised him. "I'd grunt and moan and thank you for putting your whole hand inside me. I'd be your slut."

He was finger-fucking me pretty good now. "Yes. You're very slutty. A regular tramp. You'll let me fuck you any way I want to, won't you?"

"Yes, sir."

"I'm going to fuck you now. I'm going to put on a condom and fuck this hole. Right now."

"Please, sir." My words were rattled because his hand was all but punching at my ass. "Please fuck me with your cock, Mr. Loving."

I felt Loving tremble. He pulled out and stepped away, but not for long. Soon he gripped my hips and nudged my knees wide.

Then he was in me.

It was one of the roughest fucks I've had. As I said, I'm tall, but he's big, and he's very strong. And his cock is fat. I hadn't even seen it yet, but I felt it inside me. I wanted to tell him how it stretched me, but my teeth were banging together, and I gripped the bedspread to keep from getting shoved across the bed.

He wasn't kidding about the slapping. I felt like his horse, because he kept slapping my side, trying to get me to go faster. I had been holding still until then, but I started bucking against him until I huffed and grunted.

"That's it," he rasped. "Hump me. Are you a dog? Are you a dog in heat? You my dog?" He slapped me again. "Speak, puppy."

My bark was more of a bleat, but it did its job: it made me feel dirty and fucked up, and it let him know he was mastering me. I growled and purred and grunted and barked for him every time he slapped me, until he thrust so hard I almost bit my tongue.

With a shudder, he came. I wished he could have come inside me for real, no condom, and I would've been leaking when he pulled out.

For a few minutes he lay across my back, breathing hard, and I enjoyed it, still erect, still aching. Everything from the ranch and work and life in general had gone away, and I was Loving's fuck dog, waiting to be told what to do next.

What was next was he laid me on the pillow, and as he stared into my eyes, he jerked me off. He had me pull my legs apart so my knees were on my chest and my ass was open. He tugged on my cock and stared down at me, brown eyes burning as he pumped me harder and harder.

Without warning, he said, "Come."

To my surprise, I did, and holy shit, it was huge and

thick and all over his hand and my stomach. Some of it was even on my chin. Still watching me, he fed it all to me, and I licked it off his fingers. When the last of it was gone, he traced my lips for a second with his thumb.

Bending down, he kissed me.

His tongue stole inside, and we swapped my spunk back and forth a few times. He went after my nipples again, which were oversensitive already, but he just rolled and rolled them. He drew hard on the skin above one, leaving a red mark. He left another on my stomach, then turned me over and gave the same treatment to each ass check. He put me on my back, opened my legs, and sucked on the inside of each thigh. He pushed a finger inside me, even though I was pretty raw, and I took him in, holding my legs open so we could both watch it go in and out.

When he finished playing, he withdrew and spooned behind me.

"I'd like to fuck you tomorrow," he said.

I nodded.

Though it was something I never did, with Loving I stayed the night, sleeping beside my boss, the closet kinkfest. I was full of his pinch marks and bruises and hickeys, taking a nap until I could get fucked again.

4

WE OPENED THE morning with a blowjob.

I was barely conscious as he nudged my head to his crotch, but that was fine. What was also fine was the way he swung my body around and pulled me on top of him, tucking my knees under his arms. While I sucked him off and massaged his balls, he poked at my ass again, though sometimes he licked it too. Pretty soon I squatted over him, holding on to the headboard and rattling it as he fucked his tongue inside me.

There was a mirror on the closet door, and he did me in front of it. I sat backward on his cock and bobbed up and down while we both watched. He took me to the open window and fucked me at it—nobody could see, but it felt dirty, so it got us both hot. When we finally came, it was with me on my back and my legs open in a nasty V, and this time I came first.

We took a break for a while after and ate lunch on our own.

I knew he was afraid to let me out of his sight, but I

told him he could take me to dinner. I just needed some time to myself. Mostly I napped, but I showered too. I washed my butt out more than usual because I could tell it would be an ass-centric evening, the way his mind went.

Dinner was nice. He took me to a steak place, and for a few hours it was two guys out to dinner. We talked about the ranch. We talked a fuck lot about sheep, which isn't exactly sexy, but they were getting the better of him, and well, it wasn't as if we were going to talk about him fisting me while we were in a restaurant.

But once we got to the hotel. Holy. Shit.

He had me out of my clothes and on the bed in less than a minute, I swear, but he didn't touch me, not right away. He arranged me on all these pillows, propping me up, then knelt in front of me at the foot of the bed and put my legs over his shoulders. It felt weird, and it turned me on.

Then he got the lube and went for my ass, and oh, man. Dirty. Dirty, dirty, dirty.

He played at my ass for what felt like an hour. One finger. Two. Three. One from each hand. His thumb. He had me watch it all. Some sort of sick exam. Really twisted.

I loved it.

After an hour, he went back to one hand and worked four fingers in me.

It was tight. It was hard to take, and I hissed and panted a lot. I don't know why three can be so fine and then four is a fucking missile, but it is. He held his fingers cone-shaped, but there's only so much you can do with knuckles, and he has really big hands. I wasn't ready for them.

He backed off a little, but not much. "Take as much as you can. Tell me to stop when you have to, but keep taking it until then."

So I did. He had me facing the mirrors, and sometimes he'd lean to the side so I could see how obscene it was. I was stretched so wide, not far from swallowing his hand. But I couldn't. So I took as much as I could, watching his fingers disappear inside, feeling the knuckles scrape until I said I couldn't take it.

He pulled out. But he wasn't done. Telling me to stay where I was, he went to his suitcase and came back with the longest, fattest fucking dildo I have ever seen.

"I bought it this afternoon." He greased it liberally, keeping it in front of my face. "I want to stick it in you as far as I can. I want you to see it go in. And then I want you to sit there and look at it in you for a while. Then I'm going to fuck you with it."

Damn if that wasn't what he did. We both watched as he pushed it against me, as my body sucked it in. It was as wide as four fingers but didn't have any knuckles. It felt fucking odd inside me. It went places no cock has ever been. My face was red, and I breathed hard, grunted—like I was going to shit.

He kept saying, "Good boy," sending it deeper, and I took it until it was too much.

He stopped, stood and walked away. He fucking left the room. Swiped his keycard from the dresser and went out into the hall.

I sat there for at least ten minutes, looking at the monster dildo coming out of my ass while I held my legs open. I clenched at it, held it in, marveled at it. I had about four inches yet to go before the base, but I felt so stuffed. Weird. Horny too, and I rocked a little, letting it move inside me. I wanted to touch it, wanted to start it fucking me, but I waited because this was his game. And it was a hot game.

When he came back, I was humping it hard, taking another inch or so inside me even though I felt it at my damn throat.

He knelt in front of me and held the base. "What do you say?"

My speech was so guttural I don't know how he understood me, but to the best of my ability I said, "Thank you, sir, for sticking this big cock inside me."

He turned it gently. "Do you feel it deep?"

I nodded vigorously.

"Is it stretching you?"

More nods.

"Are you full?"

Nod, nod, nod.

"Would you like me to fuck you with it?"

I groaned and started fucking myself on it.

He got rid of the pillows and lay beside me fully clothed as he plowed a huge, fat dildo in and out of me.

I don't even remember coming. All I know is I nearly blacked out, and when I got my senses back, I had cum on my stomach and my body was humming. He rolled me over, spread me, and I lay there, sated, as he used me as a fuck hole. It was so good. So, so good.

He fingered me a few times in the middle of the night. He had ignored my nipples all evening long, but he was back at them in the morning, and then we didn't fuck, just rubbed against each other until we came. We ate lunch in the room, and then we did an almost boring fuck, though it was still good, me on my knees with him jacking me as he humped me.

Then it was done. We checked out, went to our cars and drove home.

"I'm going to leave it up to you," he said as we stood outside the barn at the ranch. "I won't lie to you. I want to do this again, but I understand your reservations. So know I'm open to it anytime. You knock on my door, give me the word, and we'll pick this up. Or not. I won't look at you differently at the ranch." He rubbed the side of his neck, rueful as he added, "Though I will surely be jacking off to the memory of this weekend."

That made me smile.

But I was determined this would be all we did. I wasn't going to complicate my job. I didn't want to have to move yet, and I couldn't see how this was going to end any other way but bad if we kept on. It was going to be hard enough to work and sleep so close to him and know all I had to do was cross the driveway and there it would be, the hottest sex known to man.

I kept my resolve, and he kept his. We went back to the way we had been before Rapid City. I think I saw him a total of seven times outside of watching him ride out into the sunset, though I didn't do that as much anymore.

I worked hard. Tory was starting to rely on me about the sheep, and though I shared my dad's feelings about the animals, Loving was set on keeping them. It was never my policy to make friends with the other hands, but I was doing all right with this crew overall, better than my usual. Tory respected me. I liked the nearby town, where I went for banking and laundry and such.

Outside of a weekend's transgression with the boss and a shitty kitchen, this was an ideal setup for me.

As for Loving, he was true to his word. He didn't treat me different at all. He made no move to woo me, and I kept my distance. There was one tense moment where we were alone in his office talking about the sheep, but you would never have known a thing from watching us.

Yeah, I wanted him. I beat off to the memory of what he had done to me in Rapid City. But I was determined to be strong. I was not going to be the boss's fuck toy. I wasn't.

For four months, I did real well. But then I got the first letter, and fuck if I wasn't eight kinds of mess after that.

MY COUSIN'S NAME is Kayla, and she's two years younger than me. When I was having trouble with school, she tried to help me with my schoolwork, but she quickly became part of the problem. She meant well, but she always managed to make me feel like shit. She kept telling me I needed to work harder. Kept telling me how it was upsetting my mom and dad, how poorly I was doing in school. Half our "study sessions" were her lecturing me. I was never as glad as when she gave up and they let me drop out.

When I moved out because of the porn, she came to visit me a few times. She had gotten really into church, and she was all about praying over me. I let her do it the first time because it felt wrong not to let someone pray for you, but I don't think that was real praying. She said "Dear God" and so on, but she only talked about how nasty I was. When I said no more praying, she stood there at the screen door to my trailer and argued with me, telling me how I upset my family and how shameful my carrying on was. This was the same song and dance as Pastor, but Kayla had a way of making the barbs go deep. Usually after she left, I had to get drunk.

The thing is, she thought she was helping me. If she were a mean bitch, I could've ignored her. If she'd laughed and called me names, I could've said *fuck you* and forgotten her. But it messed me up something awful to have someone look at me with love and tell me how wrong I am. They act as if there's a Monroe Davis who is good somewhere, and I am the demon in his way. Like I have to die so he can live.

Anyway, the day I got a letter from Kayla was not a good day. It had been forwarded about four times. I opened the letter, worried something bad had happened at home, and I read it with my heart in my throat, waiting to see who had died. But that wasn't what the letter was about.

Dear Roe,

I don't know when this letter will find you or even where. But you need to hear what I have to say. Other people in the family might not have the strength to tell you what we're all thinking, but I have prayed over this, and I know this is what I need to do.

You've told me you can't change who you are, but you know this is a lie, Roe. You're going against your family, and you're going against God. You're so selfish. You don't think for two seconds about what the rest of us have had to bear because of you. You think this is all about you, but it isn't. This is about your soul and your God and your family name.

If you surrender the demons in your heart, you can end this horrible sin and get right with God. We are here in the Light waiting for you. You're off in the darkness, unaware of what Light is. I want you to call me, Roe, and I want you to come home. I will hold your hand all the way to your Salvation. I swear I will not abandon you. This is my love for you. I will pray every day for you until you come home. I won't fail, because God is with me.

This is the kind of strength I can give you, Roe. Think about that when you're alone and friendless in the dark. Then pick up a phone and call me.

Love always in Christ,
Kayla

I stared at the letter for a long time, then read it again to make sure I hadn't got it wrong. It takes me a long time to read, so by the time all this had happened, my lunch break was over, and I had to slap peanut butter on a piece of bread and run out the door.

Except I hardly ate. I tried not to think about the letter, tried to lose myself in work, but it haunted me so bad even Tory noticed something. He told me I looked like I needed a break and sent me off to take a nap.

I couldn't sleep. I paced the room until they'd gone home for the day, and then I went outside and started walking.

I didn't know where the hell I was headed. I think I was set to walk all the way to the Arctic Circle.

Jesus, her letter messed up my head so bad. I knew she was wrong, but I couldn't say why. Which made me worry she might be right.

What burned me was the way she had dogged me all the way to Nowhere. If I had still been in Algona, I could see it, but nobody knew me out here. I had good relationships with the guys at the ranch, but that's not friends. I was all about work and sleep and sometimes some TV. So if I was the kind of piece of shit Kayla thought I was, I kept it to myself. I *knew* I wasn't a shit on the job. I worked fucking hard. I put in ten to twelve hours at jobs when they asked for eight, and I did it because it's what the jobs needed.

But in her letter she took that from me. If I hadn't liked Nowhere so much, I would have quit and moved on and forwarded nothing. But I really did love my job. I'd even managed the second-rate kitchen. I didn't want to leave.

I was all jumbled and crazy and couldn't let go. So I kept on walking and walking and walking.

I was so messed up in my head, and I ended up walking too close to Loving's trail he took when he rode, and of course he caught up with me. I tried to pretend I didn't see him, tried to send off silent messages that I wanted to be left alone. But either he didn't see it or decided to ignore it, because when I didn't answer his call, he got off his horse and headed toward me.

5

"Don't usually see you out here," Loving said at last. We were in the middle of long grass, and his gelding, Chaucer, was taking the opportunity to grab a bite while we talked.

Saying we were talking is misleading. Mostly we stood doing the silence thing same as we had at the bar, though here we could enjoy a view. Nowhere was all evergreen and scrubby stuff, no big oaks because there wasn't enough water, but it was pretty. Walking on my own had only calmed me a little, but standing with Loving helped a lot more, and I didn't mind the way we stood quiet, wind playing in my hair since I hadn't brought my hat. But now Loving had us talking. So I answered.

"Not usually, no."

And we were done.

I had noticed more about him since Rapid City. Before I would have said he had sandy hair, but now I knew the flecks were actually bits of gray. He had a cleft in his chin too. I'd sucked on it and pushed my tongue in it. And when I stood this close to him, it was pretty much impossible not to think about how strong he was, how broad-shouldered, how good it felt when he gripped me and pushed into me.

But now he was talking again.

"You seem upset."

I looked away.

When he spoke, his words were halting. "Do you…want to talk about it?"

I twitched. "Fuck, no."

He relaxed, and I did too. Good. We had to be all done now. But no, he was rubbing his thumb along his jawline, and I could see him working up another bit of conversation in his head.

"Well," he said at last, "if you're looking for a distraction, I'm headed over to Crawford to catch the rodeo."

Now, when he'd said *distraction*, I admit I assumed he'd suggest sex and was all ready with my refusal. But when he said *rodeo*, I shut my mouth and thought for a minute. Lots of people, lots of noise and lots of horses.

Rough men on the horses.

You could do a lot worse than spending an evening watching cowboys straddle animals, muscles taut underneath dusty clothes as they hung on for dear life. And most of them had tents or trailers at the site, so when you got lucky and found a cowboy who liked bull in and out of bed, you could be part of another ride before you left for home.

Yep. Rodeo sounded good to me. "When do you plan on leaving?"

"Figured I'd grab a quick shower as soon as I got Chaucer rubbed down, maybe stop at the café in town to eat, then head on over."

I wasn't wild about sitting at the café with him, but I was tired of sandwiches. "Sounds good."

We didn't say anything more until we got to the fence lines, and then it was to talk about the livestock. Some of the ewes had gotten tetanus, and I did my best to explain how they could pick it up from the soil. Loving was agitated because he worked hard on nutrition, and he was after the wool on his Merinos, so it was some fine-tuning to get the balance between health and yield. I found out he had been reading up on the Internet again, which made me a little nuts.

When we were at the café, him arguing with me over what some guy said on a forum, I couldn't hold my tongue.

"Look, Loving. You aren't even telling me where this guy is from. If he's in northwestern Nebraska, it might hold some water. But I bet you money he is up in Minnesota, and I'm here to say you don't have the same soil conditions here as in Minnesota. We didn't have the same ones in Iowa. All ranching and farming is hands-on stuff. You gotta get in it to your elbows and grip it yourself before you're gonna understand it. I don't care how many books or magazines or chat rooms you toss at me. I know your soil better than they do, and that's where your trouble comes from. You gotta work with what the soil gives you. Come to grips with your own soil and your stock and make it work. Listen to your soil."

Outside of what I wanted in bed, it was the biggest speech I had ever given him, and really, it was more words than I had put together for some time to anyone.

Loving sat there listening. It was kind of a power trip, having the ranch owner so interested in what I was saying. Except when he finally spoke, all he said was, "You can call me Travis, you know."

I'd given him the best advice he was ever going to get about how to fix his sheep trouble, and all he had to say was I could call him by his first name. I grimaced and poked a fry into my ketchup.

He sipped at his cup of coffee. "So why aren't you somebody's ranch manager, Roe?"

I wiped my mouth with my napkin. "'Cause I like to move around."

"Where have you been?"

I shrugged. "Midwest. Dakotas, Kansas."

"You ever think about Colorado or Montana? Texas?"

"No," I said, then decided if I couldn't shut him up, at least I could get him to not try and get me to talk about myself. "So you ever done rodeo?"

"Only the cowboys, though not many of them either." He stared out the window. "I came to all this a little late."

By *all this* I assumed he meant being queer. I guess now it was me being nosy, because I wanted to hear more. "So did you not know?" I couldn't imagine not knowing myself, but I know for some guys it does come on like a sunset.

"Oh, I knew. But I tried to pretend. Got married. Went to grad school. Got a good job. Voted Republican." He held his coffee cup in both hands as if it were an anchor. "At about thirty I figured out I had made a mistake, so I told my wife. She convinced me to give it one more try, and I did, for six years of hell and a rack of counselors. Finally I told her, no, there was no more trying. For a while I was upset I'd wasted all that time, not only the six years but the whole marriage. But I would have hit the worst of AIDS if I hadn't gone the way I'd gone. So in a way she saved me." He gave me a funny smile. "Work with the soil you have."

I blinked, then shook my head. "I wasn't talking about women or men, Loving. I was talking about dirt. Plain and simple."

He raised an eyebrow at me. "Travis. It's not hard to say."

I pursed my lips and looked down at my plate. Damn it, I should have stayed home. "You're my boss. You're Loving or Mr. Loving."

"Tory is your boss. I write the checks and get ulcers over the mortgage." He motioned to my plate. "Are you done? Because we should head out."

"Just hold your horses." I shoveled country-fried steak and gravy onto my fork. "I couldn't eat because you've been talking my damn ears off and making me talk back. And this is too good to waste."

This seemed to amuse him, and he settled in to watch me eat. But whatever gabber fly had bit him still had its fangs in, because he started in again. "You don't come into town often, I noticed, and you don't eat out."

Whereas he ate out all the damn time, he who had a full kitchen and more than one burner. I finished my bite, wiped my mouth, and said, "Eating out is for special occasions, and I don't have no use for special occasions."

Now he out-and-out laughed. "So what is this, what you're doing right now?"

I stabbed at my food and said nothing the rest of the meal.

For a good half hour as we rode in his truck, we didn't talk. I watched the sunset deepen and felt the wind in my hair because Loving had put down the windows instead of turning on the AC.

"You aren't wearing a hat," Loving observed eventually.

I ran a self-conscious hand over my hair. "Don't wear hats when I ain't working."

"You wore one in Rapid City."

"Well, I was working then, wasn't I?"

I'll admit I said that to make him grin, and he did. He looked good when he smiled, and it eased something in me.

"So what about you?" he asked. "You ever done rodeo?"

"I did a bit when I was nineteen, but I don't care much for having my body beat like that. I'd rather chase the trailers."

"Did you go down to Omaha?"

I shook my head. "We have rodeo in Iowa. And flush toilets too."

He ignored my sarcasm and went back to topics I didn't want to discuss. "I notice you didn't list your home state in the places you worked."

I moved my eyes out the window. "No ranches. Land's too good. Got to farm it. We do cattle some, but we don't need so much pasture, which means we need less men."

It wasn't entirely true. Farms did take on hands, especially the big corporate ones. I tensed, waiting for him to point that out, and I didn't know what I was going to say. But he let it go quiet between us.

Thank God.

I DO ENJOY a rodeo. I love the smell and bustle of the circuit. It's the same smell as a ranch but with more sweat and more ass to ogle. The only trouble with rodeo is every now and again I attract girls. It's one thing for a guy to look at me as if I'm meat, but when a woman does it, I don't know how to act. I can deal with the ones who want sex, but women who see potential boyfriend material are hard to shake. I don't want to be mean, but I don't do friends of any kind, and especially I don't do it with girls.

This became a problem as we sat next to Tory and his wife and two kids, one of which was his nineteen-year-old daughter.

Tory was stout and short and hairy, but Haley was slim and tall and beautiful. She had blonde hair like sunshine, and if breasts had done a thing for me, the pretty rack in her low-cut top would've been tempting. But of course breasts and I aren't much for each other, so after I gave her a polite smile and a "Nice to meet you," I sat on an empty bench below the family and settled in to watch.

Haley parked herself beside me. "So you're the new guy."

She was breathless and beaming, telegraphing not only friendliness but interest. Both sex and friends. This was a full-on red alert, but I couldn't do my usual cut and run because this was Tory's kid.

"Yep." I kept my eyes on the rodeo.

She moved a little closer, making sure her knee brushed against mine. I wanted to see if Tory was catching all this, thinking maybe he would help me out. No luck.

"My dad says you're real smart. Says you should be a manager of your own spread." She laughed. "But don't tell him I said so because he's afraid you're gonna leave."

Well, I hadn't been planning on it, but today it was looking better and better every second. I shrugged and kept watching the rodeo.

She asked if I liked Nebraska, which I said I did. What did I think of the town? I said it was fine. She asked what I thought of Nowhere, and I said it was a good ranch. When Loving got up and said he was heading to concessions, I tried to go with him to get away, but he made me sit down and asked what I wanted.

I said, "A beer, thank you," and got ready for more torture.

But once Loving and her dad cleared out, she gave me an *oh, I get it* look. "So you're dating Travis?"

I didn't know what to do or say. I felt like she'd put a gun to the center of my chest.

She leaned over and put her hand on my back. "Oh God. I'm sorry, are you not out?"

I stood, ready to bolt no matter how pissed Tory might get, but damn if Haley didn't grab my arm and pull me down. She kept hold of my sleeve as she fished one-handed into her purse, coming out with a mint.

"Suck on this," she ordered, and I did, because what the hell else was I supposed to do?

"Okay, I've clearly stepped in the cow pie. Are you freaking out because you're straight and I said you were gay, or because you're gay and you don't want anyone to know?"

I wished to God Tory had taught his kid to whisper.

I tried again to get up, but she had iron fingers.

"Gay, then, because you would have made sure I knew you weren't otherwise." She sighed. "Relax. I won't tell anybody. But you know Travis is gay, right? He's not *out*-out, but most people know."

I thought of the many erotic ways I had been gay with Loving and nodded, keeping my eyes on the bleacher seat in front of me.

"So are you dating him or not?" Haley pressed.

"Not."

"Does *he* know you're gay?"

I tossed her a look somewhere between *shut up* and *please stop*.

She laughed. "Yeah, I'm nosy. But tell me. I don't want to make this any worse."

I didn't see how her knowing whether or not Loving knew I was gay would make any difference to anything, but I really, really wanted her to leave me alone. "He knows."

She relaxed her grip, but not all the way, and she smiled at me. "Here's the deal. Do you see the guy in the black Stetson and green button-down shirt hanging on the rail at about two o'clock?"

I glanced where she indicated and did see the cowboy she described. Tall and handsome, and if *he'd* have sat down and flirted with me, I'd already be bent over in the parking lot. But he didn't look happy about my existence. I moved my eyes to the arena. "I see him."

"His name is Cal, and he's my boyfriend. Or he was

until he broke up with me two days ago."

Well, now it made sense. "You're trying to make him jealous."

"Yes." She beamed, pleased I understood. "I think we've about done it too."

"You're telling me I should stay out of the shadows?"

She found this funny. "What? No. He's not like that."

I could see Cal just fine, and I knew he absolutely was like that.

"I think you should go over and make up with him," I said, hoping she would take the hint.

"I will in a minute." She knocked her knee against mine. "How come I had to wait all this time to meet you? Are you some kind of hermit?"

"Yes."

"Well, don't be. I'm going to tell Dad to invite you to dinner sometime, and you're going to say yes."

I should have stayed at home, even if I'd had to read Kayla's letter over and over all night. I nodded gruffly, and Haley patted me on the leg before rising and heading down the bleachers toward her soon-to-be not-ex-boyfriend, hips swinging as she went.

When Loving returned with my beer, I accepted it and sat beside him, putting myself firmly between him and May, Haley's mom. She might talk to me, I knew, but she wouldn't flirt.

I hoped to God.

Loving looked at me funny, like he was up to something. "Have a nice chat with Haley?"

I glared at him and took a big drink.

He laughed and slapped me twice on the thigh. It looked, I knew, to anyone who might have been watching us as if we were two buddies teasing. But while he teased, he gripped my leg, making me think of the way he'd held me down in Rapid City.

The touch stirred me. He didn't say anything else, but while we watched the action in the arena, his leg brushed mine, and eventually our calves pressed together. I could feel his body burning, strong and sure and achingly familiar.

I realized we were going to have sex. There was no way I was going to watch rodeo beside him all night and drink beer with him and then ride home with him in the dark and do anything besides go into his house and let him fuck me. And I knew he knew this too.

When the rodeo was over and we walked back to his truck, moving through the dark field that served as a parking lot, he put his hand on my waist, and when I didn't object, it slipped down to my ass and cupped me firmly. I felt branded, and I guess in a way I was. I was his tonight, and we both knew it.

Maybe I was some sort of demon, and maybe I was friendless in the dark. But I wasn't going to be alone, not tonight. And I sure as hell wasn't gonna be calling Kayla.

6

AFTER LOVING TURNED off the truck, he reached out and put his hand on the back of my neck to pull me closer. I didn't fight him. I opened for him before he got there, so when he kissed me, he went right inside.

We made out in the truck, sitting in the driveway for I don't know how long. He had his hand in my pants again, his fingers working up my taint toward my hole. I tried to lift up and give him better access, but there wasn't room enough for those kinds of shenanigans in the truck. We gave up and went into his house.

I had not been beyond the hall where his office was, and I got a good look at his kitchen as he hustled me through it. It was a damn fine kitchen, and I could tell from here it was going to waste. He caught me looking and mistook my reason for ogling.

"Thirsty?" He grabbed my ass with both hands. "Hungry?"

Just for you. I tilted my neck to the side so he could

have better access to it. "No."

He growled and tugged at my belt buckle, and once he had it off me, he tossed my belt off into the dark.

It'd been too long for both of us, so the first round was nothing but jerking off together on the couch, him still clothed, me naked and riding him as he held our cocks together. He fed me the spunk again, and I sucked his fingers clean, then sucked them some more because I liked it.

After, he took me up to his bed, and we had ourselves some ass.

He arranged me flat on my back, holding my legs open with my butt propped up on several pillows. He did me one-fingered dry for a few minutes. I thought he was gonna try for two, but he surprised me by going for the lube. He had me all slicked up, so I knew what he wanted to do, and sure enough, it wasn't long before I had three fingers going at me, and then we were back to four.

"You're even tighter than you were last time." He sounded pleased by this.

"It ain't like nobody's been in there since you," I replied, huffing because he was really straining me.

He pulled out a little and held still while he quizzed me. "Nobody, huh? Nothing? Not even something plastic?"

I don't have much to do with toys on my own. "There may have been a finger or two."

His grin was better in the dark. "Tell me about these

fingers."

I thought about being smart and telling him they were long and thin and attached to my hand, but he had me in the mood to please him. "I laid on the bed, spread my legs open wide, and while I jerked myself off, I fucked myself with my fingers. First one, but it wasn't enough. So I used two."

I got a kiss, long and slow and hot. When he was done, he nuzzled my neck, nipping lightly. "I can't stop thinking about fisting you. I know we can't tonight." He pushed his fingers in as deep as they could go, until I was panting. "But I want to be inside you, Roe. I keep thinking about the way you looked with that fat dildo in you. I remember the sounds you made. The way you bucked and convulsed. I want you to do it around my hand. Around my arm."

I pulled his hand out enough so I could talk. "You are such an ass man. You do know I have a cock too, yeah?"

He glanced down at my groin in mock surprise. "My God. I had no idea." But when I tried to shove at him, he brushed me aside. "Be still. I need to investigate."

Investigate it he did, chiefly with his mouth. I got hard quicker than I thought I could, but I was nowhere near ready to come again, so I was his cock-flavored lollipop while he continued to try and spread my ass. He wasn't getting as far inside me as he had that first night.

He sent his free hand up to pinch hard on my nipples, and I mean he pinched fucking hard. He had me shouting and moaning, screaming *fuck* every time. Except pretty soon it was *Fuck yeah, oh yeah, fuck yeah*, a stream of lust-fueled encouragement. I could feel his knuckles scraping me, almost inside now, my nipples swollen and pounding, my cock rock-hard inside his hot, sucking mouth. When he finally lifted up and looked at me, his eyes dark and heavy, I regarded him in surrender, naked in every way.

"You're dirty." His hand continued to work in me. "You're so fucking dirty. You'll take anything I do to you, won't you? And you love it."

"Fuck yes," I whispered, groaning and bucking my hips. "Oh fuck, but I love your fingers."

They turned inside me. "So you're an ass man now too? Or should I pull out and start playing with your cock?"

"Plow my ass. Go get your monster dildo. Fucking do it, Loving."

He looked sternly at me. He was after me to say *Travis*. I could tell. I wasn't gonna do it, though. Not even in a game. I humped harder.

"Please, Mr. Loving. Oh please, Mr. Loving, please put your big cock in me."

He bit my lip, but I had won, because he was hot for it now too. He pulled his fingers out and crossed the room to root around in a drawer.

There it was, that big fat monster. It was gonna go inside me. I squirmed in anticipation.

When he brought it to the bed, he put it to my

mouth, and I opened like a baby bird and took it in. It was so big it strained my lips a little, but I let them in until the dildo hit the back of my throat. I looked up at him and hummed on it while he carefully fucked my mouth with it. He was really fucking horny, I could tell. He wanted this same as I wanted it.

Eventually he pulled the fake cock out of my mouth. I watched him slick it up, and then I opened my legs wide as he aimed it at me. But when he started to push, I jolted.

"Easy." He kept his eyes on my asshole and kept pushing. I bore down and panted, trying to open for it. He kissed the inside of my thigh. "You are so fucking gorgeous. You can do it, Roe."

It burned like nothing else, but I kept taking it, and once he got a few inches in me, he left it in there until my sphincter relaxed. I breathed hard and whimpered, but when he started to push, my cries turned to moans.

"That's the way. Take it in, Roe. Take this big cock inside you. Pretend it's my hand. Pretend it's my fist inside you."

I arched my back and started to go guttural. I could see it. In my head I could see it, feel it. His knuckles scraping inside me, his wrist turning a little. He pushed it deeper. I was so fucking full. I started babbling as if I were drunk. My tongue felt thick, my breathing labored. I tried to say his name, but it kept getting stuck in my throat.

"Travis," he whispered, licking my ear. "Travis. Say

it. Travis. Travis. Say Travis."

"Travis," I slurred, then moaned. "Ohhhh, *Travis-ssss.*"

He bit my earlobe. "It's all in you. It's all the way inside you. The base is up against your taint." He tapped on the base, and I about went through the ceiling. "This is what it will be like with my arm inside you. *Arm,* Roe."

Tears were leaking from the sides of my eyes. I wasn't crying. I was straining hard. But it felt so good.

He fucked me with the dildo really slow, and he fucked my mouth with his tongue at the same time, swallowing my grunts and whimpers. I gave over completely to him, giving him everything in me, letting him in everywhere he wanted to go.

I'd been trying so hard to escape everything Kayla had stirred up—I'd tried to push it down, tried to pull it out, but it kept coming back. I could get rid of it all now, could give it to Loving.

Travis. I could give it to Travis.

Kinky Travis Loving who didn't know shit about sheep or soil. Who talked too much sometimes, but it was okay. I gave it all to him as he pushed his sex toy in and out of me and sucked on my bottom lip. I sank inside myself, getting away from everything, until my mind was quiet and I was okay.

I shot out, flying, flying free into the dark. I didn't land so much as I drifted down to where I'd started. When I was able to open my eyes, he was looking at me with a funny expression on his face.

He kissed my forehead. Then he walked away from the bed.

I couldn't move.

I hadn't even noticed he'd pulled the dildo out until he lifted my spaghetti legs and started wiping at my ass with a washcloth. That was about the same time I noticed I was actually pretty sore down there.

When I winced, he did too. "Sorry. I should have slowed down."

No, he shouldn't have. But all I could say was, "Mmmm."

"So you're feeling better than you were when I met you out in the pasture?"

"Mmmmm. Hmm."

I thought he was going to kiss me again, but he nuzzled my cheek instead. His lips moved to my ear, and for a second I thought he was going to say something. But at the last second he went back to cleaning the cum off my belly. It was good he didn't try to feed it to me. I think I would have drooled it out. When he was done, he rolled me onto my side, spooned up behind me and wrapped me in his arms.

Three hours later I woke up. Travis still hugged me against him, but now there was a blanket over me too.

My ass was sore. I mean, it was *sore*. I winced when I tried to roll over. I knew I wasn't hurt too bad, just stretched. Nobody was going to be fucking my ass for a few days, though, and I'd be taking laxatives to make sure we were nice and easy through the pipes. But Jesus God, it had been worth it.

I turned over and watched him sleep. His lips were curled up at the corners. So soft. His lips looked so soft.

I touched them.

I traced them.

I ran my fingers over his chin and pressed my lips against the cleft.

When I opened my eyes, he was looking at me. We stared at each other for about a minute in the dark, and then he reached up and stroked my hair.

I nipped at his chin. His throat.

He groaned.

I pushed him onto his back and started undressing him, kissing as I went. I sucked his nipples, biting a little. I ran my tongue down the line of hair leading to his groin, and I swirled my tongue in his belly button. I kneaded his belly.

He had a paunch. Just a bit extra, my mom used to call it. I made love to it, bunching it in my hands, biting at it, kissing it.

I sucked his cock.

As much as Travis is an ass man, I'm a cock man. I like to look at them, touch them, smell them, run my tongue around them. I hadn't had much of a chance at his until now. It was a beauty, I'll tell you. About eight or so inches erect and plenty fat. Cut, which I am too. I like that because then you can see all the veins and play with them. Though skin's good too because it's this built-in toy. It had the nice flat taste all cocks do, but his had this extra zing. Not really spicy. More sharp.

I sucked him all the way into my throat. I have absolutely no gag reflex, so I can deep throat about anybody. I hummed around him, and I sucked so hard my lips went numb. My tongue played hockey with itself up and down the shaft, and I coated his nest and his balls with spit. I made love to his cock like it was the last one I was ever going to see.

At some point his fingers threaded into my hair. He took to pushing me farther onto his cock, and I let him, going with his tempo now. While he fucked my face, I played with his balls and pressed my fingers to his taint. I kept humming, because I knew it felt good, and because I knew he wanted to hear me make noise. I was getting lost again. Every time I was with him, I could let go. Fucking, being fucked, sucking—I felt easy with him.

Something bumped my hand, the one at his balls and taint, and I opened my eyes. He had the bottle of lube there, cap off, fingers on the tube ready to squeeze.

I smiled around his cock. Made sense. Ass man would enjoy ass play with his blowjob.

You want to talk about tight. Tight and *hot*. God, he felt like a fever inside. Hot, soft velvet. Slick with lube. Two fingers were hard on him, but I got it done, and I snaked them deep inside and brushed his prostate. He bucked into my mouth and groaned. I did it again. And again.

I could have taken all day at the cock, but I slid my way down and sucked on his taint and licked a little at his hole. Did not care for the leftover lube, but I used more saliva to both coat my tongue and wash it away. And all of a sudden I wanted in there. I mean, *in. There.* With my fingers still working inside him, I lifted my head.

"I want to fuck you," I whispered.

Panting, he looked back at me. He was the one under me this time, all soft and pliant for me.

"I want to fuck you, Travis."

He nodded, shutting his eyes. "Bathroom cupboard. Top shelf."

I waddled on the way to the john. My ass was *really* sore. While I was in the cupboard, I put Vaseline on the outer ring of muscle. I tried not to think about my ass, tried to focus on Travis's instead as I made my way back to the bed, condom in hand.

He had been watching me and my waddle. "I did hurt you."

"Don't worry about it." I knee-walked over to him and stroked his thigh. "Can I do you on your hands and knees?"

What I wanted was to get a good grip on his ass. It was a little bit soft, same as his belly, and I had been thinking it would be nice to hold on to. I was scrawny and wiry, but Travis had a nice, plump ass. And oh yeah, it felt good in my hands.

I rode him carefully. Even without the tightness, I

could tell from his body language he didn't give his ass to just anybody. Which was a shame, because he was a good ride. I bucked into him in a sort of slow-mo version of the bronc riders at the rodeo, rolling my hips and thrusting my groin, rocking back and curving my body to compensate. I even held on to his ass cheek as if it were a pommel and raised my other hand like a rider a few times because it was fun.

Hot. Hot and slick and tight. Soft hot. Closed around me, sucking me in, taking me. I was not gonna be able to come, not a third time. Too tired, too sore. But I gave him a good hard fuck, got him all ramped up. When I reached underneath him for that nice fat cock, it was stiff and leaking. I stroked it as I thrust, talking dirty.

"Oh yeah. Yeah, baby." And it worked, because eventually he came all over my hand. He collapsed on the bed, and I rolled him over, spooning along his side. Then I kissed him, running my tongue along his jawline.

He stilled me with a touch, then let his hand slide to my neck, drawing me into his shoulder.

"I want you to tell me what you need from me so we can do this sooner than four months." His fingers brushed my hairline. "Do you need it to be a secret? Do you want to be the instigator? Only on certain days?" His hand tightened, and I could feel his frustration. "Tell me there's something I can do or agree to."

I had seen this coming in my peripheral vision all night, I guess. It didn't bother me so much because though I knew it was trouble, I wanted it too. I didn't want to date, which was what I'd been afraid he was gonna ask. But he was focused on the sex, which was fine. He was right. It saved a trip to Rapid City. And it was first-rate stuff, this. This could be fine, as long as we kept it to just sex.

But there needed to be some rules.

"I don't want any of the crew to know," I said. "Not Tory. Not anybody. I don't advertise my sex life." I stroked his clavicle. "And work is work. No fucking around while either of us is working."

"I can live with those terms." He sounded relieved, thrilled at the deal he was getting.

"I ain't done. It don't have to be only me who starts it. And you can set it up while we're at work, if you're discreet. Ask me if I'm free in the evening or whatever. I'll figure out what you mean. And you tell me about what your rules are too."

"I don't really have any requests beyond as much of you in a bed as I can get."

"Well, I got one more. I want access to your kitchen. Any time of the day."

He laughed.

I didn't. "Yeah, you think it's funny, but you aren't working in my sorry excuse for one. The kitchen is crucial to this negotiation, Mr. Loving."

He sobered a little. "All right. The kitchen is yours. Which you could have had without the sex, but you can't take it back now."

Now I did grin. "We could have sex in the kitchen."

He groaned. "Not now. If I had the energy to move, I'd go sit in the hot tub."

My eyebrows went up. "You have a hot tub?"

"I have a hot tub."

"We are having sex in the hot tub." I laid my head down. "Later."

He pulled the blanket up over us and arranged us better on the pillows. Cuddling with this man was getting to be a habit. It should have been weird, but it wasn't. I wouldn't stay like this for long because it would make my neck stiff, but it was nice.

Travis nuzzled the top of my hair, and I closed my eyes and let myself float on the sensations.

"I wish you could have seen yourself with that inside you," he whispered, mouth still on my hair. "You were beautiful. You made my teeth ache just watching you."

Right then I felt beautiful. Sore and tired and beautiful. And not lonely. Not lonely at all.

I did end up sleeping on his shoulder all night, and it did fuck up my neck. But same as my ass, the pain was worth it.

7

———————

THE NEXT MORNING was awkward at first. Lying in Travis's bed, I acknowledged work and sex had mixed a lot closer than I cared for. I hadn't made peace with it as much as I'd shoved it over because I really wanted sex with Loving.

Loving. Travis. It was getting hard to know what I wanted to think of him as. Which was why sex was always with guys in towns far away from where I worked. Why it was infrequently with the same guy. And here I'd agreed to regular sex with not just one guy but the guy who signed my paycheck.

Though I wasn't discounting that kitchen.

Rubbing my stiff neck, I slid out of the bed, took care of business in the bathroom and made my way naked down the stairs to hunt for my clothes. It was Saturday. None of the other hands worked Saturdays or Sundays, but I always checked the sheep when I got up.

I climbed into my clothes, thinking about hay and rain and yield and soil and sheep. But I saw the kitchen out of the corner of my eye and decided chores could wait a minute. I figured Loving probably had a coffeemaker, and I could use some coffee.

After so long with my hot plate and tiny fridge, I felt like I was in a palace. And it kind of was, as far as ranch kitchens went. The floor was heavy gray tile. The counters were granite, and the appliances gleamed. You could have given a bath to a midsize sow in his sink. The cupboards were sturdy, heavy wood.

But there wasn't a damn thing inside them.

He had a few cups and plates and the odd packet of noodles and sauce, and filters and coffee beans. Not much else. Normally I wouldn't snoop, but I couldn't stand it. I had to find out if the cupboards were empty all around, and by God, they were. I had more in my pantry than he did.

The coffeemaker stumped me for a few minutes. You could've launched a nuclear missile with the damn thing, there were so many buttons, and the grinder for the beans was *in* the coffeemaker. I frowned at it. It was fuss, and I don't care for fuss. Fresh beans are better, but they're expensive and troublesome, and the stuff in the tin gets the job done. But there was no can of Folgers here, only a bag of beans that I was pretty sure came from the fancy local shop. Fuss. So much fuss for coffee.

But I figured it all out, and before too long I had the java brewing. I took a moment to prepare myself before opening the fridge door, and it was about as bad as I'd feared. Eggs but no cheese. Milk, but it was expired. Beer and some diet soda. The freezer had ice cream with a layer of frost on it, a few bags of vegetables that had turned into bricks, and some steaks. They at least were from his own stock, so they were in butcher paper. I assumed he thawed them and ate them with the baked beans in the cupboard. The vegetables must've been a nice idea which hadn't panned out.

I stuffed my feet into my boots and headed out to check on the sheep while the coffee brewed.

Loving had been at this long enough to figure out you didn't just turn the animals out and watch them graze, that with sheep especially you had to get in there and trim hooves and move them around. I had them trimming more often and moving pasture twice as frequently. Tory was good about anticipating and preventing problems with the cattle, but he and Loving both tended to wait for a fire to start with the sheep before they did anything.

Which was why I had taken it on myself to check the sheep every day. They'd come to know me, and much as they didn't care for my hossing them around and pecking at their hooves, they enjoyed the alfalfa pellets I kept in my pockets, so I was still pretty popular.

When I found a wether with a sore on his leg, I lured him out of the pasture with pellets, went back for some scrub and cleaned him out good before I bandaged him. One of my goals for the year was to convince Loving to vaccinate for tetanus and other disease prevention. I'd made some calls and verified he could certify organic with some of them, but he's all about purity.

On my way to the house, I stopped by my place and raided my pantry. I carried my supplies in a Walmart sack, heading straight for the kitchen, where I planned to roll up my sleeves and get serious.

Loving was up and sitting at the counter, sipping coffee. I hesitated when I saw him. He seemed happy to have me there, but I'll be honest, I'd been looking forward to cooking alone. But that was rude, so I gave him a nod as I came through. "Morning."

I'd worried he was going to get kissy on me, but he stayed where he was, and bless him, he didn't talk, just watched me work. I poured myself some coffee and got to it.

"You were serious about the kitchen," he said eventually.

I nodded and went back to cooking.

"Omelet?" he ventured as I whisked eggs.

"There'll be one for you."

"Thank you."

The omelets weren't much. Ham and cheese with a bit of onion and pepper, bacon on the side, next to some toast. It wasn't as good of bacon as I could have had from my dad's farm, but bacon was bacon, kind of like coffee. Loving seemed to think this was some kind of gourmet feast, though.

"If you weren't so good with the sheep, I'd hire you

as a cook instead," he said between mouthfuls. "Seriously, though. Would you be willing to do this more often? I could get a line of credit at the grocery store."

"Eat your bacon," I told him. I didn't care for the idea of shopping for him. Not with his money. It was too weird, like I was his wife. Maybe I shouldn't have included the kitchen in the deal. But then I looked down at the omelet that had been so easy to make with counter space and hadn't burned on one side while being raw on the other, and I decided I could manage this if I stuck to my guns.

Thankfully he stopped talking and settled down and ate. He ate every damn bit of it. He also shooed me away and insisted he would do the dishes. I wished he hadn't, because that made me restless, so I gave myself a tour of his house instead.

It was mostly empty. He had more empty rooms than furnished ones. The living room where we had made out had a nice leather couch and recliner and had a big TV with a lot of receivers and players underneath it. Bookshelves too, with heaps of books in them.

But the other end of the room only had a fireplace, nothing to sit on in front of it. There was an empty formal dining room and another empty room meant to be a study or a small bedroom. The basement was finished, but it just had boxes in it.

One room I couldn't get into because it was locked up tight with a padlock, for storage, I supposed. In the upstairs he had three bedrooms. One had his bed, one had a guest bed, and the other was empty.

It was kind of depressing.

But there was plenty of stuff in his four-season room. You got to it through the living room and the empty room, but once you were there it was like you finally hit the actual house. He even had plants in there. A lounger, four other chairs, a rug, decorations on the walls, and lantern lights on a string all around the edges of the room.

And there was the hot tub.

It was a nice-sized unit. I don't know how many people it was officially for, but it seemed to me you could get six in there or maybe more if you were determined. Of course, the idea of being in a hot tub with six people was not something I had a personal yen for. But two guys could get in there no problem with lots of room for extracurricular activities. It was covered, so I lifted up a corner and peered underneath. The smell of chlorine filled my nose, and dark water rippled as I bumped the side. I thought about being in there with Travis and got a little bit excited.

"Go on and take the cover off," he said from behind me. I jumped and let the cover fall back down, but he came over and peeled it off himself. He folded the squares over one another and set it aside before turning to me.

He had a look in his eye that had no hints of conversation or accounts at the grocery store and everything to do about fucking me. My ass, still tender, sent up a few waves of misgiving, but my cock choked those off at the pass, pointing out there were plenty of other body parts that wanted to play.

He nodded to the open tub. "Take off your clothes and get in there."

My cock bobbed in my pants and sent out a hum through my body. "Yes, sir."

I skimmed out of my clothes and climbed into the water in under thirty seconds, then stood in the middle, waiting for my next instruction. But he only pushed a button to start the jets and waved me down. "Sit," he said, "and relax. I'm going to get a few things."

I sat in a corner, though I got up quick because the jet there was a bit too strong and went straight up my ass. Normally that could be a party, but not today. I moved around the tub, sitting in different places, watching the door. My body was humming as it anticipated what was coming.

I had not expected Loving to come back with rope.

He had a small bag too, but I was fixated on the rope. It was nylon cord cut in nice, tidy sections, which I knew from experience were just enough to bind hands and ankles.

"You didn't get out this toy kit in Rapid City," I said.

He was arranging things on a small table off to the side, but he had propped a plant up between us so I couldn't see what he was doing. "I don't bring this with me when I go cruising, no."

"This for when you and Tory feel like playing, is it?" I was aware I was the chatty one now, but I really wanted to figure this mystery out.

He stopped arranging and glanced over at me. "When I first came here, I came with a lover. It had been our plan to run Nowhere together, but he discovered he didn't have as much taste for it as I did. And I discovered I wanted to live on an isolated Nebraska ranch more than I wanted to be with him."

The careful way he spoke promised there was a lot more to the story, but I had enough to follow along. I also noted he was saying I was special, if he was trotting out these toys and fucking me here at the house. I wasn't sure how I felt about that, but this was not the time for worrying. I settled against the side of the tub as much as I could and tried to let the warm water and the bubbles relax me.

Eventually he stopped arranging and stripped down too. I lay with my arms over the edges of the tub and watched the show, feeling the hum deepening in me as he exposed more and more of his body. But before he climbed in, he grabbed two lengths of rope.

"Stand up and turn around."

I did as he told me.

"Bend over and take hold of the rail."

There were metal rails around the edges of the tub to help people get in and out. I held on to one of them, and no sooner were my hands there but he was threading the rope around my wrist and onto the rail. He tied me tight and fast with a skill that made my stomach dance.

He glanced at my face as he finished the first hand. "I still remember what 'no' means for you."

"You surprise me is all," I said. "You acted in Rapid City as if you hadn't done much of this kind of thing."

"I have, but only with one person, and we pretty much made our own rules. I don't know quite what you expect. It feels like starting over to me.

I watched him move around to the other side of me and bind my other hand. "Well, I've only played around with this stuff. There were a few tense moments a couple times, so yeah, I don't court it." He glanced at me again, and I glared. "I didn't say stop. And anyway, you're different."

"Because I'm your boss?"

No, because he was special—and the realization had my insides churning. I couldn't admit that, so I said, "Thought you said Tory was my boss."

I wasn't ready for him to grab the back of my head and come down on my mouth like he was going to take it over. It was so strong and so unexpected I sort of melted and let him dive into me. When he finally lifted his head, I was really hard.

He nipped at my bottom lip. "I'm your boss today, boy."

That made me buzz. "Yes, Mr. Loving."

He nipped me again, then ducked under my arms

and sat on the bench between them. He grabbed my hips, and I came forward to straddle him, hands still lashed to the sides of the tub. After plunking me on his lap, he let his eyes wander over me, and his fingers trailed across my chest.

"You have questions all over your face," he said at last. "I want to hear them."

Fucking hell. Him and his talking.

"Not so much questions as things I don't get," I said. "Sometimes you seem so nice-guy, and now here you are a real kinky bastard who has a bag full of toys and dreams of sticking his arm up my ass."

"You have a hard time believing I could be both?" His tone said he would have expected better of me.

"I meant you seem so innocent. And then you're so nasty." I realized I hadn't altered my statement much. "Forget it."

He kept stroking my skin, his fingers grazing my nipples more than they didn't. "That was one of the reasons I didn't want to get another teaching job. Why I wanted to do something like ranching where I didn't have to socialize." He pinched one of my nipples absently. "Though maybe I misunderstood what you're noticing. Maybe I still have more of my old guards than I know. Because I used to make sure no one could see what I thought were my dark sides. I played the game so well I sometimes fooled myself. For me sex with men always had hard edges, even when it only happened in my mind. I made love to my wife as if she were a fragile egg, but I dreamed of holding a man down and digging my nails into his skin as I pounded into him. It was easy to believe wanting men was wrong, a disease in my head."

I didn't care for him vulnerable, even in the past. "You do it right," I told him. "You're rough sometimes, and you're twisted, but it's in a good way. You make it safe to play. Safe to let go."

His eyes darkened, and he smiled. "Thank you." His hands skimmed down my sides. "So I'm kinky, am I?"

"Yep," I said. I wiggled a little.

He pinched my nipple, making me gasp. "I'm sorry. I didn't hear you."

He kept pinching, tighter and tighter. I fought for breath until I could say, "Yes, sir."

His nipple grip lessened, but only a bit. His other hand skimmed over the curve of my ass. "Kiss me, boy."

I brushed my mouth against his, but the fingers rolling my nipple started to pinch, and after a yelp, I opened my mouth and let him in. He took rough kisses from me, made me soft and willowy. I had to bend to get to his mouth, but it was so good. Our cocks bumped near each other, but I couldn't grab them and hold them together because my hands were tied. The water made everything extra sexy. It lapped around me, the foam coating our chests. Underneath my thighs I felt the hair of Travis's legs rubbing mine.

He shifted the angle of the kiss, and it turned into

this open-mouthed thing with lips and tongue. We'd come at each other with our mouths open, and then our tongues would dart out and kind of meet, and then our lips, but they never sealed. Between the kiss and the steam and the heat of the water, I felt like I might go up in flames any second.

He broke the kiss and nipped my earlobe. Then he ducked beneath one of my arms, slapped my ass with a splash before climbing over the side, and he was gone, filddling with something else in his bag.

I stood up to pull more of my body out of the tub. It occurred to me we had to be careful messing around in this hot water, though to be honest Loving didn't keep it as hot as some I'd been in. I tugged a little at my wrists, checking the knots. I really couldn't get out of them without his help. The thought sent a dark shiver through me, and I realized if it weren't Travis—

I shook my head to clear it. I kept trying to turn him back into "Loving" in my head, but it wasn't working. He was wedged in there now as Travis, the man who took me to a rodeo when I was out of sorts and fucked me raw until I was incoherent, and then he made me say his name and offered to get me an account at the store and tied me up to his hot tub and kissed me until I was weak. I wanted to say his name now, wanted to say it over and over. I wanted—wanted—

Panicked, I yelped and started to tug at my wrists again until his hands were on me, stilling me. He whispered in my ear and gentled me. On the one hand his holding me made it worse, but it also grounded me and brought enough of me back that I could calm down. When he reached for the ties to the rope, though, I shook my head.

"I'm all right." Except I wasn't sure. I kind of wanted this done now, wanted to get out and get dressed and go. The problem was part of me wanted to *go*. Wanted to give notice and be gone.

Get out, get out, get out—

I started tugging again, and this time he ignored my insistence I was fine and simply untied me. I felt relieved and miserable at once. What a fuckup. I kept my eyes off his as he helped me out of the tub like some sort of cripple, but as I tried to stand I shook all over.

My reaction kind of scared me. Was I sick?

Travis wrapped a towel around me and sat me on one of the chairs. He didn't sit beside me but across from me, wrapped in his own towel. "You want to tell me where the panic attack is coming from?"

I honestly didn't know. I swore and pulled the towel up, holding the sides together over my head. He let me sit there for a few minutes in silence, but not too long.

"Was it the rope?"

Under the towel I shook my head. I was upset because I thought of him using his first name, and no way I was admitting that.

"The water?"

I shook my head again.

The silence was heavy for a moment, and then he

said carefully, "Was it something from prison?"

I yanked the towel down fast and stared at him, dumbfounded. And pissed.

And scared.

He held up his hands. "Hey—I do background checks on the hands. Don't go looking at me like I rooted in your underwear drawer. As the guy who writes the checks, I have a right to know."

He did have a right, but it made me feel lousy all the same. I didn't pull the towel up, but I became intensely interested in the indoor-outdoor carpet underneath my bare feet. I didn't like Travis knowing about my record. Not when I had no idea what he thought I'd done or hadn't. Worse, all the times he'd seen me working hard or asked me questions he knew he was asking a guy with a record. I hadn't been hardworking Monroe Davis, the guy who was good with sheep. I had been the ex-con.

Hot shame ate at the already significant hollow part of my belly. My gaze darted to the door into the house, then to my clothes. I caught him watching me and quickly shut my eyes.

I heard him sigh, a helpless sound. "Roe, I'm not bringing it up because I care about what you did or even didn't do. I was trying to figure out why you got so upset."

My hands tightened on the towel. "There ain't no reason. It sure as hell ain't prison. Prison was fine. It was long and boring and lonely, but that's all. And I ain't lying, either. I ain't hiding anything. I have no fucking idea why I freaked out."

Okay, that was a lie. And goddamn it, but he caught it. "Roe," he said, his tone threatening.

I swallowed hard and shook my head. "Just don't, okay? Leave it. It ain't something sexy like you're thinking, some sob story about how somebody hurt me when I was tied up. It's just my dumb head." Anger came up out of nowhere, but I clamped it in my jaw. "This is why I don't stay anywhere long, and why I don't do…people."

His hand on my knee surprised me, and I jerked, but he stroked me gently, and I eased without meaning to. I looked up, which was a mistake because I got caught in his eyes, all soft and dark and kind and strong.

"Don't leave, Roe."

I glanced away. "I got to get to my place. I got…stuff. To do." Like soak my head in the toilet and flush it until I drowned or got my sense back.

He pulled his hand away, even though I knew he didn't want to.

I rose and staggered over to my clothes, climbing into them as best I could. I was still pretty damp, so they stuck to me, and if you've ever tried to put on jeans when you're wet, you know the hell I was having trying to hurry. It was dumb, because I knew he wasn't going to do anything to me now, wasn't going to stop me, but it had never been him who was the problem. It was my head. I needed to get someplace where it could explode in peace.

I holed up in my apartment the rest of the weekend. I lay in my bed all afternoon on Saturday, hugging my pillow against my chest and staring at the TV without seeing it, and on Sunday I braided about six leathers.

When I get restless, I braid necklaces and bracelets and sometimes just long rope. I learned how at vacation Bible school when I was a kid, and I got good at it fast. Everybody had me make their bracelets for them. It was all I did that week, every year I went to VBS. It was great.

Now I make leather bracelets when I need something to do with my hands. When I get too many, I dump them in the Goodwill bin. I like to make them because they clear my mind. It took a lot of them that day to get the job done, but eventually they did the trick as they always did.

Not all the way, though. The pit in my stomach wasn't quite closed, because I had realized I wanted to stay at Nowhere. I didn't want to go. Well, I did, but not as much as I wanted to stay. The thought worried me. It made me want to look over my shoulder and lock my door at night and bury my head under the pillow. I can't tell you why, but it was how I felt. But at the same time, there was this tiny little voice whispering in the back of my head, some angel saying I should stay, that everything was going to be okay.

I didn't think I was the sort who got angels talking to him. I tried to tell myself it was a tricky devil instead, but that couldn't be right. There was a peace inside that voice I didn't think a devil could fake.

So I stayed.

8

As you might imagine, Travis and I went back into a dry spell on the sex front again, and I didn't get any more quality time with a functional kitchen. I wanted to figure out how to fuck him with it just staying fucking, but I was afraid he was angling toward a relationship, and I wasn't interested.

It'd always been my plan that sex would be on the side, this thing I went and did when I really needed to. Some people need partners, and some don't. I mean, I didn't need anybody at all, and I liked it that way. I stopped having friends over and stopped going out with them to movies or to games when I realized I wanted them to hold me down and fuck my brains out. After prison, I never settled down and never got attached. No strings. Nothing to get mad about. Nothing to feel hurt over. No screwups hanging over my head.

My birthday is September 19, and I made myself a celebration by heading to the local grocery store and buying a pot roast. I had picked up a Crock-Pot a while back, and it was my aim to make a good old-fashioned beef roast with onions, potatoes and carrots. When I'd lived at home, we had them every Sunday. That was what Sunday was to me, beef or pork roast, and my family around the table jabbering after church and fighting over who'd hogged the carrots.

As it happened the first year I was at Nowhere, my birthday fell on a Sunday. Obviously there would be nobody to fight over the carrots. The roast would taste like heaven. It would be better in a real oven, because no matter what I do I can't seem to get it to cook down the way I want in a Crock-Pot. It takes too long. What you want is a slow oven, about three hundred degrees for a good three, four hours. No, roast beef should fucking not be rare. And not a word about how it is dry cooked all the way down. It isn't if you do it right. A cup of water will do the trick. Not only does it keep the meat moist, but it also makes for better gravy. Though if you want the best gravy, you add a cup of wine instead. That's kind of fussy, though.

On your birthday you get to fuss a little, so I had wine in my shopping basket. Also mushrooms. And some bread. And dessert. I mean, this was serious pigging out here. Fuss like nothing else. I couldn't wait to get home and set it all up. But just as I was rounding the corner of the bakery section and heading toward the checkout, I ran into some trouble, and her name was Haley.

She beamed at me and made all kinds of noise about

not seeing me in forever, and for a terrifying second I thought she was going to hug me right there next to a stack of canned beans. She didn't, but she did talk my damn ear off for five minutes. Asked me how I liked the rodeo. (Fine.) Was I still getting on all right at Nowhere? (Yes.) Sheep all doing okay? She'd heard I was really good with them. (Yes. Thank you.) Because it would have been rude to not ask her about herself, I asked if she was still seeing Cal.

"Oh, *him*." Her expression turned mutinous. "We were back together all right, up until last week when I found out he was seeing me *and* Lacey Sheppard at the same time. I'm done with him now." She grinned wickedly. "How about *your* love life?"

"Don't have one." I wished I had bought ice cream to go with my bakery brownies, so I could say I needed to get it home to the freezer.

But eventually she let us wander to the checkout because she was heading there too. I let her go ahead of me, and she barely stopped talking to pay the cashier. I had hoped she'd leave once she'd paid for her two-liter of soda and bag of cookies, but no, she stood there, smiling and waiting while my stuff was rung up. The cashier asked for my ID, and I pulled out my wallet and passed it over.

The cashier scanned the license and did a double take. As he passed it to me, he smiled and said, "Happy birthday, Mr. Davis."

I knew then and there I was fucked.

"Oh my *God*, your *birthday?* Why didn't you say?" She looked at my supplies. "Birthday dinner for two, is it?"

If I had thought for a second I could have said yes and gotten rid of her instead of getting the third degree, I would have. I shook my head. "Just enjoying a quiet night at home," I said, trying to emphasize *quiet* and *enjoying*.

No dice.

"What? Are you kidding me? You can't be alone on your birthday."

"Been alone on my birthday for about five years now. Suits me fine."

But Haley grabbed my bag along with hers and herded me out the door toward the parking lot. "I have to go to a hair appointment, but then I will be over to the ranch, and I will pick you up and take you to dinner. We'll paint the town red. It's karaoke night at Sid's Place and live country music at The Bronco, so you decide which one you'd rather, and we'll do it. Or we could do both."

"I don't want—" I started to say, but she cut me off with an aggressive kiss on my cheek.

"No arguments. Around five, okay? *Yay.*" She did an odd little dance in front of the cart corral before hurrying away. I was still standing there dumbfounded when she scurried back and handed me my bag she'd inadvertently run off with. "Bye," she said, kissed me again and took off.

I was really upset about this, and instead of putting the roast together when I got back, I paced the small length of my apartment trying to decide what to do. I didn't want to go. But how could I tell her? Even if I got her to actually listen, she'd be upset. I mean…shit.

In the end I decided to put the roast off until the next day and let her take me out to dinner, but that would be it. I'd pretend I was sick or something, but she'd probably try to cook me soup. I took a shower, got dressed and sat down to braid some leathers. I got so lost in them I forgot the time, and the next thing I knew there was a knock on the door.

"Wow, you've really spruced the place up." She waltzed in and did a turn around, taking it all in, but she stopped when she saw the leather I had taped to a chair. She picked it up, holding it like it was a bird that might fly away if she moved too much. "Oh my God, this is beautiful. What is it?"

I wished I had put it away before I answered the door. "Just braided leather. I do them sometimes. It's no big deal."

"Are you kidding? This is incredible. I mean, you have six rows in this, and a pattern, but it sort of crisscrosses." She turned it over a few times, captivated. "Is it a necklace or a bracelet?"

I hadn't decided yet. "It's nothing."

"Well, if it's nothing, then I want it when you're done."

At first I thought she was making fun of me, but she

kept looking at me expectantly, and I realized she really wanted it. "Okay."

"Great." She let go of the leather and offered me her arm. "Shall we go?"

Of course we had to run into Travis in the fucking stables.

He was saddling Chaucer up for his evening ride. He seemed damn surprised to see me with Haley. Who of course spilled the beans about why she was over.

"Your birthday, is it?" He lifted his eyebrows at me. "I had no idea."

"I *know*," Haley said. "I only found out because I was in front of him in the checkout when he tried to buy wine. Travis, he was going to spend his birthday all alone. So I'm taking him out. Dinner and a bar crawl."

"Sounds good," he said, wistful.

For a horrible second, I thought Haley was going to invite him along. But before she could, he finished cinching the saddle and gave us a tip of his hat. "You two have a fun time."

There are three restaurants in town, but she took me to the same café Travis had. I considered having the country-fried steak, then thought about the hot roast beef sandwich, since that was close to what I was going to have. But I planned to make the roast for the next night, so I kept getting stuck.

"You should have a steak," she told me. "I am. They're good here."

It did sound good. It was expensive, but again, it

was my birthday, and I wasn't having the night I'd planned. Likely she'd try to pay for it, and I knew I couldn't pick it.

Resentment over having my quiet night ruined boiled over. I was having the steak and paying for it myself. When the waitress came and took our order, I told her so before Haley had a chance.

"But this is your birthday," she protested as the waitress left. "You shouldn't have to pay."

"You are not buying me a steak. You should be spending your money on college or something."

That made her grin. "I'm at WNCC right now, but I hope to transfer to UNL second semester this year." When I blinked at her, her grin widened. "Western Nebraska Community College and University of Nebraska at Lincoln."

I nodded and sipped at my coffee. "Good for you."

"Where'd you go to college?" she asked me.

"Nowhere." Something perverse made me add, "Didn't finish high school."

Her eyes got real wide. "How come?"

Should have figured even if I shocked her, she wouldn't stop asking questions. I shrugged. "Didn't suit me."

"Did you ever take the GED?"

I shook my head.

She kept on. "But why not?"

"'Cause it don't matter."

"But in this day and age, and in this economy especially—" She cut herself off, but I got wary at the expression on her face. "I'm going to help you get your GED, Roe."

Jesus God, it was Kayla all over again. I attempted to look stern. "No."

But damned if she didn't stop being a nineteen-year-old and suddenly turn into some kind of Amazon warrior. "It isn't that many classes, and you can do it online now."

"I ain't got a computer."

"Travis does. And I do." She held up a finger at me. "Don't give me this line about how you don't need it. If you can look me in the eye and tell me not having your high school diploma hasn't made life harder for you, I'll let *you* buy *me* dinner. If not, you have to give me a better reason than *I don't need it.*"

It *had* been trouble at some ranches. When a lot of guys were looking for work, they took the best. I don't know why proving you could sit still and parrot shit from a book for four years made you better, but apparently it did. I picked up my spoon and twirled it in my fingers. "It just ain't for me. There's something wrong with my head. The words all jumble around, and I get itchy. I can't learn a thing by reading. I've always been that way."

This only seemed to excite her more. "There's nothing wrong with your head. It's a learning-style issue. You're a tactile learner. A strong one. It makes sense with how well you do working with your hands. You probably have strong sensory experiences all around. You probably notice smells and colors and lights more. What about auditory? If something is read to you, can you understand it?"

Where was all this coming from? I blinked. "Sometimes. But it's better if I can see it and do it."

She was nodding, looking like I was some prize she'd discovered. "Seriously, Roe, you have to let me help you. Because this is what I do, or what I want to do. My brother had trouble in school too, and Dad and I helped him. And we got the school to read him the tests, and some of them they had to rewrite so he could show them he knew instead of doing multiple choice. Now he's graduating."

She was so excited she bounced in her seat, and eventually she reached across the table and captured my hands too.

"Oh, please. You should have seen how upset Bart was until we got the school to change for him. He thought he was so dumb. They wanted to put him on Ritalin, but my mom said no way. I know some kids do need it, but it wasn't what was right for Bart. He needed the school to change to how he needed to learn. I'm going to go to college, and I'll be a teacher, and I'll be the best teacher there ever was. I'm going to make a difference, and there will be kids like my brother who go to college because of me."

She was a fucking force of nature. I swear she could glare at a tornado and make it suck back up into the sky in shame. She didn't think I should be ashamed. She believed in me, and I have to say, when she looked at me, I felt like maybe I wasn't dumb and messed up in the head. Hell, for half a second, I thought maybe I could go to college too.

"You're gonna be a good teacher," I told her at last.

She beamed at me and squeezed my hands, which were still trapped in hers. "Can I start with you?"

If a tornado didn't stand a chance, there was no way I was gonna last.

But I got a bit of my pride back in the end, because when the meal was over and the bills came, I picked up them both and paid them, and when she tried to object, I said, "It's my first payment for the lessons."

It was worth it to see her grin. Deep down I knew her lessons were never gonna take, but part of me tucked away some hope too.

I WASN'T ABLE to plead sick and get home to my brownies and bottle of wine. In fact, I didn't try. It was fun to hang out with Haley once I got used to how intense she was. We started at the bar called Sid's Place, where I steadfastly refused to sing any karaoke, so of course I ended up singing it anyway. Haley laughed and clapped and hooted, and so did a few other people. I threw in some air guitar too for good measure.

She was really sweet. She even deflected the girls who tried to flirt with me by hanging on my arm. I was nervous at first that she was coming on to me, but when she started murmuring in my ear about which guys had the hottest asses, I relaxed. She did know how to pick them too. One of them I thought, maybe, was giving me the eye. But I wasn't into that, not tonight. Okay, I would *like* to be into that tonight, but I was having fun with Haley. The cowboy could wait.

Haley dragged me to the stage a few more times for karaoke. I was up to six beers by then, but she was stone-cold sober because she'd had nothing but Diet Pepsi all night. Said she was my driver and that was her job. She started picking up my tab too, but I decided I would get her back later.

She had a real thing for the Dixie Chicks, and I think we hit every song of theirs on the machine. I always did enjoy singing, especially the harmony, and I knew the songs, so it was easy. The audience whooped, and I laid into it, hamming it up like hell, even swiveling my hips a few times. I don't know quite what had come over me. I think between the alcohol and how off my usual this was, the parts of my brain keeping me in line didn't know what the hell to do.

Though when I caught sight of Travis in the back of the bar, all my guards went up.

Jesus, but he looked good. I suppose he was the same as always, just a nicer shirt and black jeans and his tan Stetson, but holy shit. I couldn't look at him. I knew he would be able to see everything, and so would everybody else. We were singing a song now I didn't know as well, so I had to focus on the words and try to anticipate the melody and the harmony both. It was hard because all I could think of was Travis listening to me sing, watching me. I made it through the song, but when it was done, I told Haley I needed to take a break.

Travis came over to our table, and of course Haley told him to sit down and join us.

She might have been right about me and the sensory stuff. Oh my God, the scent of him wrapped all around me, and not just the splash of cologne he had put on. I could smell his skin. I remembered what it tasted like too, and even with all the beer, I felt the memory on my tongue. I tried not to look at him, but I kept stealing glances. He was always watching me too.

I began to wonder if this was going to lead to sex again. I hoped it would.

I should have figured Haley would pick up on what was going on between us. She chatted Travis up, but I could sense the plot forming in her brain. This time I actually kind of wanted to cheer her on.

Eventually we moved on over to The Bronco, Travis beside me as we walked down the sidewalk. When I staggered, he righted me, and after several stumbles he held on to my arm. His grip was strong and sure, and it made my head spin. I knew I should get home and get to bed because I had to work early in the morning, but I didn't want to go. Not without him.

The Bronco was a lot darker and dirtier, but it was rowdy and crowded, and best of all we had to squeeze together into a booth. Haley once again made sure it was me in the corner and Travis beside me. She left us to go get drinks, but Travis didn't move over. He stayed pressed up to me, letting me feel his heat. I felt his hand on my leg too, and I wanted to purr.

"Last time we sat in a booth like this, things got really interesting."

I leaned into his ear. "I want you."

His hand slid higher on my leg, pulled it open on its hinge, and when his hand cupped my cock through my jeans, I pushed into him, showing how much I wanted him.

Then Haley came back to the table, and I blinked, attempting to come out of the spell.

His hand stayed on me, working me, making it almost impossible for me to focus on anything. Though I wasn't so gone I didn't hear Haley say, with pride, "I'm going to help Roe get his GED."

Travis kept up his wicked massage underneath the table. "That's great." Didn't sound surprised at all I didn't have a diploma. I suppose he looked it up when he was checking out my prison record. Surprised he didn't look up my birthday too while he was digging for all my secrets.

They began to make arrangements for us to meet at Travis's house, using his computer, but I couldn't pay attention because of his damn hand. Eventually I couldn't take it anymore. I undid my fly and guided him in there. I was so hard, and I was slick too because the head kept weeping, and he'd sweep it up and slide it over the shaft. And meanwhile he was asking Haley about her summer job at the nursing home and about her mom and her brother.

But it must have been getting to him too, because all of a sudden he said, "I really need to be heading home." He squeezed my cock.

"Me too." *I need to go have sex.*

Haley, I hope, did not know about the hand job, but she knew code when she heard it. "I thought I might pop back into Sid's quick. Do you mind taking Roe home, Travis?"

"No," both of us said at once. And from her grin, I knew later I was going to get quizzed about how my night was, but I didn't care. I sure as hell hoped it was going to be great.

9

"So it's only been a month this time," Travis observed as he angled his truck out of the parking lot onto the road. "It's a step up, I guess."

"I wanted it," I confessed, emboldened by the beer. "I just wasn't sure how to phrase it."

"What you said in the bar works fine, for the record."

The beer didn't only embolden me. It made my tongue loose. "But I don't want any hearts and flowers. I'm not a relationship man."

"Is that what had you panicking?" He cast a sidelong glance at me. "How the hell did you get me wanting a relationship out of tying you up to the side of a hot tub?"

"Actually, it was the grocery store account."

"What? You think that's a relationship? I was trying to bribe you into cooking for me. So you're saying I should have offered a rough fuck instead? All right. I'll write it down."

"Are you mad?" Damn stupid loose tongue.

"Exasperated, yes. Mad, no." He gave me another look across the seat. "Monroe Davis, you have some twisted thinking going on in your head. I already figured out you don't want a relationship. That's why I keep giving you a wide berth. I could tell if I tried to make friends with you, it would spook you, so I thought maybe we'd just fuck, since we did it so well. But I have no idea where to put my foot when I'm around you. I seem to scare you off no matter what I do."

He made me sound like such a headcase. Maybe I was. "I don't do friends."

"Everybody has friends, Roe. It's part of being human. Anyway, you were doing all right with Haley. What do you call that?"

I had no idea what to call Haley. "She's a stubborn filly."

"Word of advice: don't call her a filly to her face unless you want your ears blistered." He smiled. "You looked good, singing with her. I never knew you could let go that way."

Me either. In fact, now that I was starting to sober up, I felt awkward about it, like I'd exposed myself too much. Talking about it was only going to make it worse, though, so I found a patch of silence and wrapped myself in it until we got home.

The road from town to Nowhere was narrow, and I realized I hadn't experienced it in the dark until now. The joke is Nebraska is flat, which sure it is, especially where they put the interstate. Which makes sense if you think about it, because the flatlands would mean the least amount of work putting in four lanes of road. But western Iowa and Nebraska have plenty of hills, if you go looking for them. I mean, our farm back home was nestled in the hills and had a little creek bed running through it.

The hills around our farm were full of trees, and I don't care if it was spring or summer or fall or winter, that place was so beautiful sometimes it hurt. The way the sun cut across the land, the way the grass rippled in the wind, the way all those thick green leaves sounded when a gust blew through—there's nothing else like it. I don't care what you try to show me, what ocean or mountain. There's a beauty to a quiet place you can't get anywhere else.

During the day you could see the hayfields rolling on either side and the scrubby brush and grass in the ditch. A dry creek bed wound around the east side of the road, eroded deep and full of gnarly roots and rocks and mud from the last gullywasher. The fence below marked the edge of the cattle's grassland. The road was gravel, single lane, and it was one of those with grass growing down the middle. The road rippled and rolled over the hills all the way to the outbuildings and the sheep pasture and the tree line taking you out to the ridge.

In the dark, though, all you could see was black and the gravel and sometimes the branches of trees or brush along the side of the road. It felt like we were driving into nothingness that kept expanding just in time for us to get there. I was supposed to be sitting braiding a leather and listening to the radio with my belly full of roast, but instead I was full of beer, throat raw from singing at the top of my lungs, riding along with Travis on the way to the ranch in the dark to go have hot animal sex. The world was spinning and strange and wild, and in that moment I felt wild too.

I said, "I want you to tie me up again."

He glanced briefly at me. "That didn't go so well the last time."

"I know. That's why I want to do it again." I turned and looked at him, taking in his profile in the glow of the dashboard lights. "I told you then. It wasn't the tying up that did it. It was my head."

He didn't say anything, just kept watching the road. So I pushed.

"Come on. You know you want to." When he didn't answer even then, I started to lose some of my confidence. "Well, unless you don't want to."

"Oh, I want to."

His voice was quiet but weighted, slithering around me and making me still.

I wasn't sure what was going to happen when we got to the ranch, so I tried to let myself float, tried to let the darkness swirl around me and make everything go away. It did, but I was very aware now of Travis beside me, of his hands on the wheel. I was aware of his scent, of cologne and beer and the stale, vague smell of bar clinging to us both. I remembered the other times we'd had sex, remembered the feel of his big arms. I wanted him and everything he might do to me so much it scared me a little. It was the same want that made me run the last time, but I tamped it down. I wasn't going to make an idiot of myself. Not this time.

It started out well enough. By the time we pulled into the drive, my blood was already humming. I sat in the dark, silent cab, waiting for his lead.

When he reached over and put his hand on my leg, I opened for him. He ran his hand up the seam of my fly, traced the outline of my erection with his thumb. When he undid the fly, I lifted my hips to help him. When he slid my jeans and underwear down over my hips, I quivered, but I held still and let him take my cock in his hand.

So close. It was so close in the cab of the truck. I could feel his breath on me. I could feel his hand on me. I felt the clinging vinyl under my ass, felt the rough brush of denim against my thighs. His cologne was a fog around me now, and I could smell sex: sweat and precum and cock, my cock, stirred up by his hand. I knew this was only the opening act, knew I would face tomorrow sore and raw and spent, and I was ready. Ready for rough. Ready for the ride.

I was not ready for his kiss. I could have handled him grabbing my chin, forcing me open and diving inside. Hell, he could have spit into my mouth, and I'd have shivered. But it wasn't that kind of kiss.

He came in slow. He had his eyes on me the whole time, hard and strong, which was the only thing keeping me from turning away. Until the last second I thought he was going to do something kinky, like bite me or lick my lips. That would have been fine. But after he bent down, my unsteady breath against his mouth, he kissed me. Soft. Sweet. Unbearably gentle. It made me feel jangly and strange. Made me ache, made me hurt. Made me want to turn away, and I started to.

He opened his mouth over mine, sealed our lips together and stole inside.

Not forced. He snuck in there. Teased his way in. When I started to fight him, he lured me back. When that became too much, I tried to pull away, but he dragged me onto his lap.

He kept kissing me, kissing me deep and tender, but his hand molested me with a roughness that gentled me. Real quick I figured out if I wanted dirty, I had to give him sweet. If I kissed him back, if I let my mouth fall open and my body go soft for him, and above all if I didn't flinch away from tender, drugging kisses, he would nip at my chin or pinch my nipple or let his hand slide along my taint. He had me feeling so crazy. Any second I was going to blow up, nervous and excited and uneasy all at once.

Eventually he stopped kissing me, and he spoke into my ear, whispering and nuzzling, all the while with his hand working me over below.

"The thing is, much as I want to fuck you, much as I want to tie you down and get out the crop and smack you until you're beet red all over your body, I can't shake the feeling the more we do this, the more likely you are to leave Nowhere. If I take you to rodeos and out to dinner and invite you to use my kitchen, pretty soon I'm going to be looking for another ranch hand who knows something about sheep." He paused for a beat, his finger at my opening. "You want to tell me I'm making this up?"

Fifteen minutes ago, this discussion would have made me feel panicked and trapped, but all I could think about was how if I was good, I could get that damn finger. "I won't leave."

The finger teased but didn't enter. "You lyin' to me, boy?"

"No, sir." I shut my eyes and tried to press down on him. "Please."

"I've got your number, cowboy. You just want a fuck. You want an escape. You want a job, and you want some sex on the side, maybe. You'd rather the job and the sex weren't in the same place. But they *are* in the same place. I want to be your lover, but I want to be friends too. I'm not asking you to move in. But yeah, I expect you to take care of my cattle and sheep and occasionally have a conversation with me as well as let me tie you up and fuck you blue. You man enough to deal with that, or are you going to run as soon as we finish tonight?"

My head was spinning, and my body ached, it was so taut. But Jesus H, he had my balls to the wall. *Man enough.* He'd said it on purpose to get my goat. This was *bullshit.*

But it was good bullshit. He had me dead to rights, which was why I answered him honest. "I don't know."

His hand at my shoulder gentled. "I say you are."

I shook my head, keeping my eyes shut. "You don't know me well enough to know that."

He chuckled. "Oh, I do. Better than you can imagine. And I say you can cowboy up and do this, Roe."

I didn't answer, just stood there as he stroked the sweaty skin of my neck. When he nipped at my ear, I shivered, but when he spoke, I went still.

"You're worried I want to make you my lover? Well, I don't want one, Roe. I don't want a partner. I don't want a husband. I want a boy. I want a little slut I can order what to do. I want you in boots and spurs and chaps and nothing else, sucking on my cock with a tail hanging out of your ass."

When he bit the soft flesh of my lobe, I went slack.

"I want you to work for me and cook for me and talk with me. And then I want to fuck you, Roe. I want to fuck you so good I ruin you for anybody else. I want to make you mine. *Mine.* I want to brand you like the cattle. Not because I'm in love with you. Because I want you, and because I don't want anyone else to have you."

I went through so many mental somersaults while he said all that to me I lost track of what I actually felt.

Relief. Fear. Hope. Terror. Arousal. Disappointment. Joy. Suspicion. I didn't even have a clue as to what triggered what. I felt it all in waves coming one on top of the other. I had no hope of speaking. I was waiting for him to demand I say I wasn't going to run, and I was terrified because I knew I couldn't promise it. Then he'd be angry, and this would be over, and then I'd have no choice but to leave—

The thought made my chest get so tight I hunched forward against the pain.

He grabbed my chin and tipped my face toward his with a force that made me open my eyes and look at him.

We were tangled on the seat, my jeans sagging down, my shirt rucked up and half open. I figured we were like some clutch on one of those romances my mom bought at Walmart, except Walmart was never going to have two guys. I never read any of those books, but I'm pretty sure the heroes never wooed the women by swearing they were just after them for sex and a sense of ownership.

But I kind of felt like one of those women on the covers anyway. Nobody had ever held me this way. Gripped me like Rhett Butler and demanded some kind of accounting out of me. A couple of guys had tried to ask about having a relationship, but it had been a hesitant asking, which had terrified me as much as the word *relationship*. This wasn't any asking. This was claiming.

I wasn't sorry. I felt like that crazy sea inside me was settling into a calm. He had drawn it out of the bottle I kept it in, but when I looked up at him, it eased, because if my wild insides were a sea, his gray eyes were the world's biggest fucking bowl, and they held me. Caught me and held me and bore me up.

I eased back, lifted my open mouth to his, and I let him claim me, let him inside my mouth, relaxed my ass even before he pushed inside there too. I let him have me, and for the first time since I could remember, I made love to a man without thinking of how I was going to get out of it or how I was going to give us some distance once we were through. I let him have me, let him make me feel good.

And oh, yeah. It was so good.

HE TOOK ME to the horse barn, to the stalls underneath my apartment.

There were about fifteen stalls but only three horses. The horses we hands used were all out to pasture next to the sheep. The other stalls were empty.

He shut me in one.

Travis took my hands and placed them on the grill beside the door, and he tied my hands to the bars with stout rope. He took care to wrap it around my wrists at my shirt cuffs so it didn't chafe, but he tied it tight. I wasn't getting out.

Then he dropped my jeans to my ankles and gave my legs the same treatment, spreading them as wide as the denim would allow. After that he swatted my ass and left.

He was gone a good twenty minutes. I stood there, blood humming, cock at half-mast. We were gonna fuck. I mean, we were gonna *fuck*. The roughness of the rope he'd used excited me. The cooler evening air against my bare ass reminded me how exposed I was and made me want to hump at the wall.

He kept me waiting on purpose, I knew, but it didn't freak me out at all. It made me more eager. By the time he finally did come back, all I wanted to do was suck on various parts of his body to show him how fucking happy I was with this. But then I saw what he had hoisted over his shoulder.

It was some sort of fucked-over bench. Part wood, part metal, part cushion, it had been designed and fashioned to someone's particular details and not by an expert hand. To my mind it looked just right for leaning over while you got your ass reamed.

Fuck, yeah.

I craned my head around to watch as he set it up in the middle of the stall. He was setting up beyond my line of sight, which I figured was on purpose. I could hear him clicking and banging on things, and I saw several flashes of rope, but I couldn't tell exactly what was going on. Then, with no warning at all, a knife was slashing the ropes holding me, and I tumbled backward into Travis's arms. I shivered from surprise and anticipation, but he held me close a second and said,

"You okay?"

I nodded, then on horny impulse, turned my face to kiss him.

I stopped at the last second, realizing in this game I had to ask for that sort of thing. I let my eyes do the asking, though my lips did part in hope.

With a growl in the back of his throat, he caught my mouth in a hard kiss full of tongue. He took hold of my cock with his bare hand and jerked me a few times, making me moan into his mouth. His tongue slid deeper into my throat, and I let him in as deep as he wanted to go. But when he withdrew, I didn't chase him, only held still and waited until he told me what I was supposed to do next.

What he did was bend me over the bench and tie me to the ropes he had rigged up on all the sides of the stall before lashing me to the bench too.

He had clearly put a lot of thought and care into this arrangement. He'd dragged some sort of platform out from under the hay and set the bench on it, and before he tied me down, he made a few adjustments to the legs. He was tailoring it to my height, but he wasn't putting all his trust in it, either. That was what the tying me to the stall sides was for. Mostly they were supporting me, but the bench was taking the stress off my lower back. I figured in a few minutes it was also going to be keeping my ass where he wanted it, but right now it was support and cosmetics.

The ropes, though, were ones he'd brought from

the house. They were nylon and designed specifically to be gentle on skin. You can tell the difference, and as one who is frequently acquainted with them, you appreciate the difference too. They kept me spread wide-open, trussed and helpless, but they didn't cut. I was all skin now, because as he'd removed the first rope, he'd removed my shirt too, and my jeans and my underwear.

My boots he put back on. And he slapped a cowboy hat on my head. It was kind of a nice one, a chocolate-brown felt, so dark it was almost black. All I had was a straw Stetson for working. It didn't rain much out here, but nothing fucked up a nice felt hat like a downpour. Felt was for show.

Well, I was showin' now.

Travis didn't waste any time with words and got straight to the fucking. He kept his clothes on while he inspected me, running his hands all over my naked body, careful to avoid my asshole and my cock. He did pay some attention to my mouth, sliding his fingers inside. They tasted like rope and leather, and I sucked on them hard, running my tongue around them as they fucked me.

I looked up at his face from beneath the brim of the hat and let him see how much I liked it, hoping he could see how much I wanted his cock in my mouth too. For a second I felt really proud of myself because his eyes went dark, and he brought his crotch up close to my face. I nuzzled eagerly against the denim. But all he did was pat my cheek and pull away, and then he was gone.

He went around to the back of me and had a party in my ass.

First he rimmed me as I have never been rimmed. No warning, no stroking, not even telling me—he pulled my cheeks apart and dove in fast. And by in, I mean he went *in*. His tongue fucked me like a cock. When I flexed, he slapped at my ass cheek, which made me jump, so he slapped me again. Pretty soon he was licking and sucking and fucking and slapping, all as hard as he could. I humped the bench and moaned, hoping he would never stop.

His finger came at me with no warning, and after three pumps, he pushed a second one in alongside. I gasped and cried out because it hurt a little. But he kept pushing, so I kept taking, panting until the pain became a burn and then pleasure. I took him in dry until he got tired of it, and then I waited to see what was next.

It turned out to be a big, fat dildo with a tail.

He showed it to me first, and he had me suck it. It was purple and ridged, getting very fat at the base, but mostly what impressed me about this was how long it was. Well, that and the horse tail hanging down. But mostly as I took it into my throat, feeling it press alarmingly deep, all I could think of was how far that fucker was going to go into my ass.

He smiled at me as he used it to fuck my mouth. "You're going to be a pretty pony," he told me. I shivered, because he sounded wicked. It was hard to believe this was the nice guy Haley had beamed at in the bar, the fine upstanding rancher everyone in town admired. Right now I couldn't imagine him teaching anybody anything except how to suck on a purple silicone dildo.

When he pulled it out of my mouth, he greased it in front of me, sitting on a stool. He took his time.

"Where is this going to go, boy?"

"My ass, sir," I said, not taking my eyes off it.

He kept up his work. "How far is it going to go in?"

"All the way, sir." I shifted my hips against the bench in anticipation.

"And then what will you be?"

"Your pony, sir."

He smiled. His hand stilled at the side of the dildo, which was thick with grease, as was his hand. He looked almost sadistic. He made sure I saw how much he was enjoying having me like this, how much he was going to enjoy ramming the dildo into my ass.

I let him see how much I was going to enjoy having all this done to me.

The dildo was rough to take, rougher than I thought. Those ridges were a trick, and by the time he had it halfway in, I was grunting and panting. But he didn't let up, didn't stop, and so I kept taking, and the next thing I knew, I felt the fine hairs of the tail brushing my taint. He slapped my rump once, making me jump. Then he came around to my red, sweating face and held something up to my mouth.

It was a bit.

It was of some sort of soft material that didn't puncture when I sank my teeth into it but did give, which meant it would absorb the shock. The thought I was going to need shock absorption really fucking turned me on. But best of all were the leather leads attached to each side of the bit, and Travis gathered them both in his hands and pulled them around my head.

He also let me see the crop in his hand. I shut my eyes and moaned softly in anticipation.

"Keep the bit in your mouth, but if it gets to be too much, spit it out and tell me to stop. If you can't for some reason, shake your head no. Other than that, I'm not going to stop. We're going to ride, pony. You're going to ride this bench hard and fast, and I'm going to hold your lead and whip your fine ass the whole way. Nod if you understand."

I nodded eagerly, though I didn't quite understand how I was going to ride the bench. I assumed he meant I was going to dry hump it like a dog.

Holy shit was I wrong.

There was a hole in the side of the bench I hadn't known was there until Travis slid my cock into it. I was a little worried at first because I thought it was going to chafe like fuck, rubbing against wood, but then he guided my cock home, and I moaned around the bit. Jesus. It felt the same as fucking into an ass. It was even warm like one. He had one of those flesh things lined up at the hole, one of those fuck-tubes. He wasn't kidding about fucking the bench. I thrust a few times because it felt so good.

The crop came down hard on my lower back, and I yelped around the bit. He whipped me until I stopped thrusting.

"You wait until you're told, pony."

I hung my head, ashamed. I should have known better.

He lifted my hat and stroked my hair. "There now. You hold still, and when I tell you to giddyup, you start riding. Understand?"

I nodded and tried to nuzzle his hand.

He let me, and then he put my hat on. Keeping hold of the lead, he positioned himself behind me. He spread his thighs so I could feel his jeans on my legs. He kneaded my rump affectionately with his hand. Then he pulled the reins tight and hit the other cheek firmly with the crop.

"*Giddyup.*"

I giddyupped. I thrust my cock into the bench and let the dildo fuck me as the tail swished at my taint. I moaned and grunted as the crop came down on my ass, first one side and then the other. I went faster. I nodded my head and bucked my hips and imagined I was galloping over the fields, carrying Travis wherever he wanted to go.

He never stopped beating my ass with the crop. There was no playing around, no nothing nice about it. This man was hardcore. He slapped the leather on my cheek with a force that wasn't only going to be red. It was going to welt. He got so into it he pulled back, straining my neck on the reins and moving away from my thighs as the crop whizzed through the air, all the while shouting *hee-yah* and *come on, boy, faster.* I fucked and grunted and moved my hips in time to his will, and I let go.

I let fucking go. I was his pony. I was his boy. I was his.

When he brought me down, it was abrupt, but I held still and tried to follow what he wanted me to do. He cut me free at my hands, but my legs he kept tied down, only adjusting the slack on them. I clutched at the bench, holding still as he worked. When he removed his shirt, my heart quickened as he draped it over my shoulder. I watched as he took off his boots and his jeans.

I wrapped my arms around his neck as Travis put his hands on my shoulders, kicked the bench aside and tossed me into the hay.

On the way down, he grabbed his shirt and draped it around my ass, taking a second to make sure the flaming, wounded flesh was protected. I could still feel the hay poking through the cotton fabric, but the gesture of protection touched me so deeply I didn't care.

He trussed my legs, opening me wide, reattaching the rope to a bolt in the stall. I watched as he put on a condom and slicked himself with lube. I moaned as he pulled the dildo out of me and tossed it away.

I raised my arms and looped them around his neck as he pushed inside my body and rode me again.

I forgot I still had the bit in my mouth until I tried to kiss him, and when I realized it was there, my eyes widened in surprise. He grinned at me and removed it, then grabbed hold of my jaw.

"Open," he told me.

I did. And I moaned as he came inside, fucking me with his tongue as he fucked me with his cock. When he stroked me, I came with three tugs, I was so turned on.

He, God bless him, took his time, riding me until I was squirming, until I was whining like a dog beneath him. Then he pumped into me with four hard strokes, and he came too.

I wished he were coming inside me for real. I'd never let anybody do that before, but I wanted it then, and I wanted it bad. I wanted to feel his spunk leaking out of me. I wanted to feel it fill me. I wanted him to plug me up to make me hold it for him. The thought shook me, but it made me go soft in his arms too, made me melt against his sweaty, hairy chest and kiss his neck.

He grabbed the hat, which had fallen off, and slapped it on my head. "That's your present. Happy birthday."

I laughed, and my smile lingered. It was still there when I tipped the hat rakishly and lay on the hay, sated and satisfied. I smiled at him until he bent to me and kissed my mouth, soft at first, and then hard. I shifted against his shirt, letting him swallow my quiet moan. The hay poked at my welts as he settled between my thighs, rubbing his sticky cock along mine while his fingers sought my hole.

I wasn't able to go to work at all the next day, and I couldn't ride a horse for a solid week.

It was pretty much the best fucking birthday ever.

I COOKED FOR him the next day and a lot of days after.

We had my roast for dinner the day after my birthday, cooked in his oven. He went up to my place to get the stuff, because I really was a sore motherfucker after he was through with me. What I liked was he never got bent out of shape about it. He just asked if I was hurt, and when I said yes, he tried to apologize, but after I shook my head, he nipped my shoulder and quietly took care of me.

Honestly, we almost went too far, and it's to his credit he felt bad about it. Technically it was his job to make sure it didn't go too far, but the thing was, it wasn't *really* too far. But as he took care of me later that night and the next day, I watched him carefully, and I figured out why it upset him so much.

"I don't mind a little soreness now and again." I lay on the floor on my stomach, propped up on my elbows as I sipped the coffee he'd brought me. "Nothing chases the monkeys out of your head like a sore backside."

He sat on the floor in front of me and grimaced into his mug. "Riley—the student who came here with me.

He would tell me he was okay when he wasn't." He traced his finger around the rim. "In and out of bed."

I lifted my eyebrows. "Student?"

He gave me a sly, not-very-apologetic grin. "He was a grad student. He wasn't in any of my courses, but he was still off-limits, technically." He shook his head, smiling in memory. "All he had to do was say, 'Yes, Dr. Loving,' and I was lost." He reached out and stroked my cheek. "That was his bench. We made it together. But he was shorter than you are, so I had to make some modifications."

I liked how he was touching me so gently. "But he didn't care for it out here, you said."

"I was angry when he left, but in hindsight, I suspect it was all he could do. We said we were all about commitment and honesty, and in the end we were both lying. He didn't want to be here. Didn't want to build a ranch with me. A life, yes—but he wanted the life we'd had in Omaha, the life I'd hated. He wanted a nice house and parties. People coming over. Snuggling on the couch." He frowned. "Well, it's not that I don't like those things. I just—" He ran his thumb along my lip. "He wanted the relationship, wanted the cuddling and soft words and flowers. And the same as he didn't tell me he wasn't happy, I didn't tell him either. The only difference is I faked it longer than he did."

I wanted to promise I wouldn't lie to him, but I couldn't, so I kept quiet. It felt good, lying there with my ass burning so bad I couldn't stand anything but ointment on it, warming my hands with a mug of coffee as Travis stroked my lip. Quiet. I loved the calm and the quiet and the easy.

After a few minutes, though, I broke the silence myself. "I got to get back to making dinner."

That made him smile, and he watched me as I cooked wearing nothing but a dish towel for an apron. He sat at the table, sipping coffee. Watching my ass. "Jesus, but I whipped the shit out of you, didn't I?"

"Yep." I slid the onion I'd been cutting into chunks into the roaster pan I'd sent him into town to pick up. He'd fussed, wanting to get me a fancy one, but once I'd heard they had the cheap, black, tinny thing with white speckles like my mom had, I wouldn't let him come home with anything else.

"It hurting you still?"

I shrugged and reached for the bowl of mushrooms I'd washed. "A bit." I glanced over my shoulder and give him a dark grin. "Kind of like it."

The look on his face made me shiver. "Goddamn, Roe, but the shit I want to do to you makes my balls ache just thinking about it."

I turned back to the roast, trying to keep my cool, but my cock was getting hard. "Give me a few days, and you can help yourself."

I knew he was coming over to me because I heard him pushing his chair back. I still jumped, though, when he put his hand on my shoulder.

"If you run…" he said, then let the sentence hang

unfinished.

I shook my head and stared down at the roast. "I ain't gonna run."

His hand tightened against my bare skin. "You do, I'll make the tanning I gave you last night feel like a little kitten licking your toe."

That would probably kill me, so I knew he was exaggerating, but it made me feel soft inside. Nervous, but soft.

It's hard to explain. It was kind of a hope, but with jagged edges. When his hand tightened further, I realized I hadn't responded, so I nodded, then with some effort, I turned and nuzzled his jaw. Then I went back to cooking dinner.

I didn't run. I don't know what exactly had changed, but something had, and it made me feel easier than I remembered feeling for a long time. This was just a convenient fuck, but we were friends of a kind too. Friendlier than I'd ever been with anybody since…well, since ever, I guess. But it was okay, because we were only fucking.

Not so much that first week, though. We sucked each other off a few times, but we didn't fuck proper until four days later, and even then for the next week it was pretty vanilla stuff. I could tell he was watching me careful, wanting me to heal, yeah, but also not quite believing I wasn't going to freak out. I didn't, though.

I cooked for him quite a bit. First the roast, and then I did some pork chops and some steak. I found out the way to Travis's heart was a casserole. Scalloped potatoes about had the man coming in his pants. He was a real pleasure to feed, I'll tell you. Soon I was cooking for him every night.

Despite us both being careful, other people were starting to notice how often I was hanging out in the boss's house. I was pretty sure several of them knew there was more than cooking going on. The other hands didn't say anything, but Paul, the hand who had been with Nowhere almost as long as Tory, watched me extra close whenever Travis was around.

Haley knew, obviously, and she clearly approved. She took to coming over for dinner on Tuesdays and Thursdays and hung around to give me my GED prep. I asked if her mom minded, but she laughed and said her mom thought cooking was unwrapping a pizza or emptying a can.

I know she didn't say anything to her dad, but Tory seemed to have picked up on Travis and me as well. Probably what tipped him off was the way every time he came in at the end of the day to give Travis his report, I was in the kitchen. It took him a few days, but eventually he came in and asked what was cooking. That day it was meatloaf, as I had a yen for it. Meatloaf and baked potatoes and candied carrots. Tory gave me a look which threw me for a second. I'll be damned if *please let me eat your dinner* wasn't a lot like *please let me fuck you.* Not something I needed to see in my ranch manager, but what the hell.

I invited him to stay for supper, and I hadn't finished the sentence before he'd whipped out his cell phone to text his wife he'd be home late.

In bed that night, I told Travis about it, and it made him laugh.

Now, don't go getting ideas. I hadn't moved in or anything, but a lot of times I stayed after for a fuck. Not every night, and sometimes I left to be in my own place for a while before I came back for some fucking. That night I stayed at the house, largely because Tory lingered after dinner. We sat around the table and drank beer and talked about cattle and sheep.

They sidetracked into politics, at which point I went to do the dishes. They're both Libertarians, and they get all worked up over *government intervention*. Never mind the subsidies they sign on for every year.

I don't care for most politics. In my mind they're all messed up, but I don't see how giving the big companies more freedom would help anything. I don't say a word since Travis is a fucking doctor and I didn't finish high school. I figure I don't have much right to say anything.

I made the mistake of saying this to Haley.

"Why the hell wouldn't you have a right?" She closed her fist over the laptop and pursed her lips. "Did they say that to you?"

"What? *No.*" I held up my hands. Jesus. "I meant I ain't educated like they are."

"There are plenty of complete idiots walking around

with postgraduate degrees. There are plenty of really smart people who don't get half as far as you are right now."

That I doubted, but there was no way I was winding her up more than she already was. "Well, I ain't arguing with Travis or Tory. It's a waste of air."

She laughed. "See? You're smart."

Thing was, Haley kind of made me feel smart. She was going to be one hell of a teacher, some sort of bright version of Kayla. Instead of making me feel shitty about myself and making everything worse, she made it all better. Once she figured out how hard reading was for me, she had me doing everything in audio, and when she could, she did demos.

My favorite was when she explained molecular structure. She had this kit which reminded me of Tinkertoys, and she had me build molecules. My test was I had to label them and show them to Travis. I felt kind of silly, but he turned out to be a good teacher too. He listened carefully, and he gave me praise. He didn't make me feel like I was some dummy he was patting on the head.

I wouldn't let him teach me math, though. Haley said I should, but I wasn't having any of it. It was bad enough I was such a fuck-off compared to him. I didn't want him to have to see how bad I was at what he went to school for.

The essays were hard, and at first I figured they were going to be what broke me. But Haley wouldn't give up.

Her computer had a built-in microphone, and she made me talk them out before she had me write anything. She gave me all these key phrases she said I could use over and over again. She also put outlines for my essays on cards and had me arrange them in pieces across the kitchen table, building paragraphs out of squares and rectangles of different colors, and damn if all of a sudden I didn't understand how to put an essay together.

Best, though, was her list of phrases. They were anchors. There were *starting words* and *connecting words* and *list words*. It was almost a puzzle. Between them and the outlines on rectangles, I only had to plug in the bits and there it was: an essay.

Also, she kept doing this thing with a hamburger. Something about how the essay was like a burger, with a bun that was the same at the beginning and the end, but the meat and the good stuff was in the middle. The bun held it together. She had me map out my essays on the burger—my first one was on sheep—and then I'd look at the burger while I talked. It was a good strategy, and it got me over my nerves. By the end of October, she had me writing short ones down. It really was not hard.

I got cocky and decided to play with Travis a bit.

One night, after I knew he was in bed, I went over to the house. He looked so good sitting in bed with his shirt off and his glasses on while he read a book I just about gave up and jumped him, but I had worked for an hour on this, so I cleared my throat, held up my paper, and I read what I had written.

Why Travis Loving Should Fuck Me
by Monroe Davis

I think Travis Loving should strip me naked, tie me up and fuck me until both of us are crazy nuts and come our brains out. The reasons I think this should happen is because sex is fun, because we both enjoy it with each other, and because there are several things we haven't done yet.

Sex is considered fun by many people. Sex can relieve stress and lower blood pressure, even though at first it raises it a little. Tension is also relieved by sex. Having sex can make someone less irritable and can make conflicts seem less important. Sex can help people be more creative too. There are many different ways to have sex, and finding all those ways out can be fun.

I personally enjoy sex very much, and I know Mr. Loving does too, because I have had sex with him many times. He should have sex with me again because we are actually really amazing at it together. I have had sex with many other men, but never as long as I have had sex with Mr. Loving, and I keep having sex with him because he is just that good. Also, maybe it is bragging, but I think if he says somebody else gives him better head, I think he is lying.

The final reason Mr. Loving should have sex with me is because we have left a lot of territory unexplored. For example, I know he has some wicked spreaders in the basement, because I found the key to his locked room, but he hasn't used them on me yet. Also, I have frequently wished he would fuck me while we watched some of the porn I found in his cupboard. Thirdly, he made all this noise about fisting me and then never did anything about it.

As you can see, there are many reasons Travis Loving should fuck me. Sex is fun, we enjoy it with each other, and there is a lot more sex we could be trying. I hope you have learned a lot from this essay, and I hope once I stop reading, Travis Loving will bend me over and fuck the shit out of me.

Halfway through reading the thing I started to feel silly, and my face got really red. At first I had felt all clever, and to be honest, I was proud. This was longer than anything I'd written for Haley. But what had seemed so clever when I was punching it out on the laptop she'd loaned me seemed dumb when I was reading it to Travis. I mean, I was using all her phrases, and I had the hamburger thing down and the thesis statement things, but my essay sounded like a fourth grader had written it. I kept on reading because I figured it would be less stupid than quitting midstream, but instead of leering and winking at him when I was finished as I'd planned, I stood there, chest hurting, waiting in agony for judgment.

I thought maybe he'd laugh or smile or tell me I was nuts. I was hoping for it, actually. But he didn't do any of that, and he didn't look at me like I was strange, either. If anything, *he* seemed strange. He stared at me for a long time, and about when I was ready to bolt, he took off his glasses, set them on his nightstand and motioned to me.

"Come here," he said.

I went.

He took my hands in his and pulled me onto the bed with him, making me straddle him. For a long time he still didn't say anything, and I had to fight to keep from squirming. I started to worry he would say something serious because he had that look about him. I felt like instead of making a joke, I'd somehow turned everything really serious.

But all he said was, "Are you heading anywhere for Thanksgiving?"

That made me blink and draw back a little, but he held me fast. I shook my head.

He kept his eyes on the center of my T-shirt. "I was hoping I could talk you into cooking. Maybe we could ask Tory and his family to come over." He cleared his throat. "But it's just an idea."

"It's a good idea," I said. "Haley's hinted at it, telling me how they have some turkey loaf thing her mom buys in the freezer and cooks until it's a brick, and how she bets I make a mean turkey."

"Do you?" He looked hopeful.

"I haven't ever made one," I confessed. "But I always wanted to try."

"Get me a list of what you need, and we'll do it." His hands skimmed up my arms. He still wasn't meeting my gaze. "Didn't realize you were so fixated on fisting."

The way he was stroking my sides was starting to make me horny. "Well, you can only play so much pony."

"It's just that your ass looks so good with a tail."

A tail and cane stripes lately. He enjoyed watching me make up excuses to Tory why I couldn't ride. But honestly, even that had been a month ago now. We had been so busy we'd mostly stuck to quick fucks, between my GED lessons and Tory hanging on for dinner and the actual ranching.

I leaned forward, making his hands slide up my body. "Course, my ass might look even better with your hand shoved up inside."

He pulled me down and held me tight, so tight I almost couldn't breathe. He kissed my neck, nuzzling it with a tenderness that almost broke me.

"Jesus Christ," he whispered, and he shook a little.

A thousand butterflies blew up inside me, but I shoved them down and shut my eyes, pressing my forehead against the side of his head. When I was able, I whispered, "Roe. Just call me Roe."

He laughed. His hands relaxed, and he pushed me onto the mattress and fought with my clothes.

That wasn't the night he fisted me. But I was plenty sore in the morning.

I stopped caring that everyone else pretty much

knew what was going on. I mean, I cared, but I didn't let it rule me. It was too hard to hide how happy I felt when I saw him crossing the yard and he waved at me. I couldn't hide my grin when I headed toward my car to run an errand and he stuck his head out of his office and told me to go get my damn hat. I got tired of trying to make sure nobody heard me talking to him about groceries or asking him if he would print off my homework for Haley. Nobody else seemed to care. Three days before Thanksgiving, Tory hired a new hand, and I heard him asking Paul what was the deal with me and Travis.

"He's the boss's man," Paul had said, like he was reporting the weather. The new hand had been surprised, but he hadn't pushed it, and he didn't look at me any different either, outside of minding his p's and q's around me, as if I might report him.

I decided it was a good thing. I was the boss's man, making Thanksgiving dinner for him and the ranch manager and his family. Why the fuck not.

I was really happy right then. I was happy all the way up until the day before Thanksgiving, the happiest I'd ever been, each day better than the one before. Then the second letter came and reminded me I didn't have any fucking business being happy, not now and not ever.

10

THIS TIME THE letter wasn't from Kayla but from Bill. Never in ten thousand years did I expect to get a letter from my brother, and when I saw his name in the return address, everything inside me went still.

I only have the one brother. Mom had six miscarriages, two before Bill, two between us, and two after me. Eventually the doctor said there was no way she would ever carry again. She cried when they told her because she really wanted a girl. I remember still how much she hurt over it. I was seven, and I stood in the shadow of the hall, listening as my dad comforted her. "I'll never get my girl," she kept whispering, like her heart was breaking. She rocked back and forth on the edge of the couch, keening. I didn't realize I was crying with her until Bill came and took me to our bedroom to go to sleep.

I lay in bed staring at the ceiling a long time. My chest hurt a lot, my stomach feeling like I hadn't eaten in three days, though I'd polished off two pork chops and a mountain of potatoes at supper. It was like I'd sucked up my mom's sorrow, and I couldn't seem to let it go.

I said, "I wish I had been a girl for mom."

Bill's reply was gruff. "She'll be all right. Go to sleep, Roe."

I'd lain there all night, though, praying to God. I asked him to make me a girl for my mom. I prayed harder than I had ever prayed. I did my best to explain to him it wasn't fair for my mom to want a girl so much and not get one. I asked for a miracle birth. I asked for him to change me. I asked for a baby to be left on our doorstep in a basket—a girl baby. I tried everything I could think of.

When I finally went to sleep that night, I dreamed I walked up to heaven and met God himself. I couldn't see him for all the clouds, but I could tell he was there. I knew I was supposed to ask him about my mom, but I was so overwhelmed I just sort of stood there. And somehow it was enough. Standing there before God, it all felt okay. I knew then it would all be fine. It was beautiful. So beautiful.

Then the clouds parted and a man stepped out. At first I thought he must be Jesus, but he didn't look like the paintings at church. But beautiful wasn't enough of a word for what he was. Looking at him made me ache, and it was the opposite of the feeling I'd had listening to my mom cry. It hollowed me, but it filled me up too. I cried out and ran to him, needing him, wanting him, knowing once I held him everything would be okay, always, forever. The light got bright, he took me in his arms—and then the dream was gone and Bill was shaking me, telling me it was time for chores.

Bill was always the good brother. He had no trouble in school. He did sports and dated the right girls, and the farm was going to be his as soon as Dad retired. Before they kicked me out, everybody figured I'd work for him, and I was fine with that. The only thing Bill hadn't done by the time I'd left Iowa was get married.

Now here was a letter from him. For twenty years I talked to him every day, and then I didn't speak a word to him for five. Now here was an envelope full of words. My brother's words.

My mail comes to Travis in the office. Normally I don't get anything but my cell phone bill and an occasional catalog. Since I started hanging out for dinner, he has taken to leaving my mail on the kitchen counter where I will find it, and that's where I found Bill's letter. I was actually coming into the kitchen to lay out my battle plan for the next day when I saw it, and so I read the letter in Travis's kitchen.

Dear Roe,

Kayla has been after me to write you this letter for a month now, and I decided since it was coming on Thanksgiving, I should sit down and do it.

I hear you are in Nebraska. You don't know how good it feels to know where you are. I hope it is in a good place with friends. I hope you are on your way to healed and ready to come home to us.

Mom is good, but it's getting hard for her to get around the house because her arthritis is so bad. Except they aren't sure if it's arthritis exactly. She has all this pain all the time, and they say it might be nerves. Sometimes I catch her crying at the sink. At first I thought something had upset her, but honestly I think it's just the pain. We've taken her to the Mayo Clinic twice, but they don't seem to know anything.

My wife is helping. I guess you don't know about Sarah, do you? She's a real pistol. You'd like her. I hope someday soon you get to meet her. We're moving in with Mom and Dad. Sarah got laid off last week, so it works out. She hasn't been a farm wife, and I'm a little nervous about my two women in the same place. I have the feeling Dad and I will be hiding out in the barn a lot finding things to fix.

I guess I have to tell you about Dad. Last year they told us he has Parkinson's. He wasn't shaking so much, but he shuffled when he walked, and sometimes he had trouble with his coffee cup. Now it's pretty much full-blown. It's coming on faster than it should. And it's bothering Mom, because she did all that carrying on about no stem-cell research, but now they say it's the only thing that could provide a cure, and it's never going to come in time for him. It's hard to see him break down like this. Every day there is more he can't do.

I looked it up, and they say the next step is demen-

tia. I don't know how I will face watching Dad lose his mind. The hardest days are when I have to tell him he can't do something. It seems so wrong to do that to Dad, but if I don't, he'll hurt himself or worse.

As long as I am giving you bad news, I might as well give you all of it. This is something I haven't told anyone, though Sarah has told her mother and her sisters. The fact is Sarah and I can't have kids. And the problem is me. I guess I shoot blanks. That's been hard to swallow. It's hard to write. Sarah wants to tell Mom and Dad, but I don't want to. I don't want to tell them I can't give them the grandkids they want. Mom has been knitting pink baby hats. She has ten of them. She wants to knit them now while her hands still work. She asks me every other day when I will give her a granddaughter to put one on. I can't bear to tell her there won't be one. We're looking into adoption, but I know it won't be the same.

I hope you will write back. Hell, I hope you will come back. I hope you get this and come home. I want you here. I probably should have said so when you were still in town. Sometimes I wanted to, but I wasn't sure how.

I'm asking you to come home now. To come home and help with the family. There will likely be some rough edges, but I promise I'll fix them. I hope you are all healed. I hope this time away has eased things within you. I hope this can be okay. I hope you have turned away from bad sexual choices. I need my brother, Roe. I need you the way I have never needed you before.

Call any time. Any time at all. Or just come home. We're all still here.

Love from your brother,
Bill

When I quit reading and looked up, it was as if everything had changed around me. I put the letter in my pocket, but it was thick and heavy there, and no matter what I did, I could feel it burning me. I kept working because I had to, because I was making food for everyone and they were counting on me, but my hands shook while I did it.

Like my dad, who had Parkinson's. Like my mom, whose hands hurt, but who was knitting hats for granddaughters she was never going to have.

Ten minutes ago everything had been good, but now it was all wrong. I had never wanted to run more in my life, but there was nowhere to run. The stuff chasing me was in my head.

Home. Bill wanted me to go home. On the one hand, I wanted to get in my car and go now. I wanted to drive all night until I got there. That he'd asked me made my chest so tight every few minutes I had to stop and put my head down on the counter to gather enough strength to stand again. But even as it hurt to hear about the trouble at home, and as it moved me more than I thought it could to hear Bill ask, I could feel the shadows on that letter.

Hope you are healed. Hope you have turned away from bad sexual choices.

What upset me was even as the letter had me wanting to go, those shadows made me want to stay. Turn my back on my brother. And it chilled me to the bone, because what kind of bastard lets hurt feelings get in the way of family? But mine were in the way. And I knew, much as it tore me up, I couldn't go home.

I couldn't cook, either. I had come to the kitchen to lay things out for the next day, to rinse and brine the bird with the recipe Haley and I had found on the Internet. Now I was having a hard time telling my left from my right.

Run.

Goddamn it, I needed to run so bad it was a knife in me. But I couldn't. Couldn't go home. Couldn't run. Couldn't cook. Could only stand there, bleeding out but never dying.

It was the pot that did it. Travis had bought me this big-assed stockpot to soak the turkey in, and I was trying to take it to the sink when I dropped it because I was shaking so bad. It made this huge clatter on the floor, and as I reached down to pick it up, it was dented on the side. Fifty fucking dollars the thing had cost, and I'd ruined it.

Same as I ruin everything.

Travis says when he came in I was making this funny howling sound and smashing the bottom of the pot onto the tile. He had to wrestle it out of my hand. All I know is I felt like my insides and outsides were rotten. There is this kind of sick scum you get on the bottom of a horse trough, and I felt like horse-trough scum, body and soul. I wanted to die, I really did. If I'd been all on my own, it might've been bad.

But Travis was with me. He dragged the pot out of my hands and hauled me to the table and put me in a chair. He tried to call the doctor, and I told him no and swore a blue streak at him. He yelled back, asking what the fuck did I think I was doing, and if I didn't calm down right now he was either calling the hospital or the cops. I could take my pick.

I didn't want anything more to do with prison, and hospitals scare the crap out of me, so I shut up. But of course he kept asking what had happened, and what the hell was I supposed to say? I'd have ducked out, but he'd have followed.

It was the hardest thing I'd ever done, but I reached into my pocket, and I gave him Bill's letter.

If I'd thought I'd felt rotten before, it was nothing on sitting there waiting for Travis to read. I wanted to get up and do something, to make coffee or fuss, but when I tried to get up, he held me in place with a hand on my arm, and so I stayed put.

As his eyes moved across the page, I tried to guess what he was thinking, but he has a pretty good poker face. Anyway, I was too nervous to read him.

There was this nasty voice whispering he was going to tell me to get out, that he was going to hate me. It said he was going to think I was a real asshole. Ask what the fuck I was thinking, leaving my family like that, and then he'd ask why I hadn't left for Iowa already, and I'd have to tell him I didn't think I could go—

The world got black for a second, and the next thing I knew Travis was shaking me and shouting. Except he wasn't mad. He was scared shitless. I guess I had forgotten to breathe there for a few minutes and had passed out.

We moved to the couch. He pressed a glass of water into my hand and made me drink it, but he kept a hand on my knee as he finished reading. I don't know why his touch helped so much, but it did. His hand was warm and strong, all his strength coming into me.

He put the letter down in his lap, stared ahead for a few seconds, then laid it on the coffee table and turned to me.

The world got fuzzy and dark.

"Roe," he said, sounding tired and sad, "stop holding your breath."

I let the air out and sucked more in. Things got instantly better. "Are you mad?"

I felt my face go hot as he blinked. "Mad? Why would I be mad at you?"

"Because of the letter." I pointed at it and glared at him. "What else?"

Now he was all wary and careful. "Roe, I'm not sure why you'd think I'd be angry at you because of that letter. Clearly it was upsetting, but why would I be…"

He paused, then spoke as if the thought had just occurred to him. "Do you think I'll be angry if you need to go home?"

I shook my head and stared at the carpet beneath my feet. "I can't. I can't go home."

I waited for him to hate me.

But all that happened was we sat there for a few awkward minutes, and then he groaned and sank into the couch. "Shit." He sighed and rubbed at the side of his face. "Roe, I'm sorry. But I'm going to tell you right now I really, really don't do this sort of thing well."

I turned and frowned at him. "What thing?"

He looked almost green. He gestured vaguely at the letter. "This. Talking about stuff."

"I don't want to talk about anything," I snapped. The anger carried me all the way to my feet, and even though I still felt wobbly, I paced back and forth between the couch and the TV. "Jesus Christ. You think I want to talk about this letter? Did I ask you to talk about it? No, I did not. I shouldn't have fucking showed it to you, but the hell I was going back to prison."

"Roe, that was a joke," he said, and then I really lost it.

"Prison ain't a joke. And neither is the fucking hospital. I don't want to see either again, ever. I don't want to see you either, if this is the shit you are going to do to me."

That seemed like a good exit line, so I headed for the door.

Fuck it, I *would* leave. This was a joke anyway. The happiness I had been feeling was a lie. I should go. I had a pile of money from staying so long in one place and Travis buying most of the food, and I'd go. Go and get drunk and fuck. Go as far as I could, and I'd get another job, and this time I wouldn't let there be any way anybody could find me. I would go. I'd go right now.

I didn't make it to the hallway.

He grabbed me around the waist, and when I tried to fight him, he pulled me back and wrestled me to the floor. I kicked and clawed and swore, but he held me down. He pressed his body against mine and held me to the carpet while I shouted and cursed and tried to fight. Held me until I stopped fighting.

I turned my head to the side and stared at the far wall, at the bookshelf with all Travis's books lined up there. I was tired and numb, and I lay there, waiting to see what would happen next.

Eventually he said, "I may have done this poorly."

I closed my eyes and willed him to shut up.

He groaned, shifting his weight along my body, and then he laughed, a funny, sad sound. "Riley would laugh his head off at me just now. He'd say this is exactly what I deserved."

I willed him to shut up harder.

"Explain it to me, Roe. Explain why you don't want to go home."

I opened my eyes but didn't look at him. "Because it won't work. They want me to be a Roe I can't be, and it will only hurt everybody more if I go back. But it's hard to hear him asking and not answer."

It seemed so damn simple when I said it like that.

"Who's the Roe you can't be?" he asked.

I was still staring at the wall, but it was fading, turning to gray mist. "Straight."

His sad sigh ripped me up almost as much as the letter did. "I'm sorry."

I gave a curt nod. But when he brushed a kiss on my cheek, I shut my eyes.

"Do you want me to call Tory and cancel tomorrow?" he asked.

That brought me out of my funk in a hurry. "No. I said I would cook. I want to cook." I tried to sit up, but the room was spinning, and I had to brace my hands on the floor to keep from falling over. "I just got to get my bearings."

I felt his hand on mine, and all the strength came rushing back. "Let me help you."

No, I tried to say, but the same part of me that wouldn't let me go home kept my mouth shut and had me nodding.

He did help me. He was a real good help. He helped me get organized and basically kept my head from wandering off. He wouldn't let me get worked up over the stockpot and pointed out you could still soak a bird in it with a dent on the side, so we did. He helped me put the oranges and things in with the brine, though he did leave the damn stickers on half of the fruit. He carried it to the fridge and shoved everything over to make room for it.

After helping me organize my recipes for the morning, he made me get in the hot tub. We didn't talk, only sat there and soaked. It felt good. And after, he took me to bed.

I had thought I wanted a rough fuck, but it ended up being tender, just rubbing cocks with a lot of kissing. Afterward we lay stuck together, the semen drying like glue between us, which usually he hates, but tonight neither of us had the will to move.

Eventually he said, "I haven't done anything but send my mom Christmas and birthday cards for five years. And my father died with the last words between us being him telling me to get my stinking faggot ass out of his house."

"I don't even do cards," I confessed.

"Is that easier?"

I shrugged and stared up at the ceiling. "Dunno."

"You were close to them? Before?"

I nodded. "When I was twenty, they found me out. It wasn't pretty. I tried to stay around town, but that was how I ended up in prison. When I got out, I left."

"And kept moving. So they couldn't find you, or so you didn't get attached?"

I couldn't say anything to that. It made me feel funny, the way he said it. Kind of shitty too. And lonely.

He laughed softly. "You really do hate talking."

He looked funny in the dark, his face all full of

shadows. "I'm trying to do right. Trying not to hurt anybody. Trying to stay out of trouble."

I felt fluttery and strange when he stroked my cheek. I shut my eyes, swimming in the feeling. It went on a long time, though, and when I opened my eyes again, he had the damnedest expression on his face. You would have thought I had used the crop on him well past *no*.

"If you need, now or ever, to go home, I don't want to be in your way." His fingers fell on my lips. "But outside of that, I'd rather you didn't leave." His thumb stroked my chin and he added, "Ever."

He looked like he was going to be sick now. I frowned at him. "You okay, Travis?" I asked.

"I don't know," he whispered. "Are you going to run?"

I tried to prop up on my elbow to get a better look at him because he made no fucking sense at all, but he reached up and grabbed my arm so tight it hurt.

I figured it out.

Yeah, for a second, I panicked. But I was getting used to these two parts of me, the fluttery top part felt guilty and wanted to get away from Travis, and the part underneath seemed to have a better handle on every-thing. It held me in place until I calmed enough to speak.

"So you're telling me you're getting serious on me?" I said at last. "That this is more than fucking after all?"

"Roe, you sleep in your own bed at best once a week. Your toothbrush is here. You get dressed in your apartment, and occasionally you shower or go over there to 'get some space.' This has been more than fucking for months now."

I lay down and stared at the ceiling. I should have been scared, but somehow I wasn't. Surprised, yes. And yet, not really. I thought about how the idea of leaving had torn me up, about how my feet hadn't so much as itched since forever.

"Well," I said at last. I shook my head.

He did not let go of my arm. "Roe?"

I turned my head and gave him a severe look. "So what is it you're suggesting, exactly?"

He got pissed again. "I'm not suggesting anything. I'm saying you had better not fucking leave."

"Who said I was leaving?" I thought of my birthday whipping and his threat after. Hadn't we already had this conversation?

Apparently we hadn't had it enough, because he was serious. "You get this look about you sometimes. If I go into town, I spend the whole time watching to make sure your car doesn't peel off down the highway. They've figured out to sit me near the window at the café. I just know one of these damn days I'm going to come back, and you'll be gone, and I'll have no fucking way to find you. It makes me want to tie you up in my basement and never let you out, ever."

I tried to pry his hand off my arm. I didn't say anything because I didn't know what to say. It had never occurred to me somebody would get bent out of shape over me leaving. I wasn't sure how I felt about it, either. Good, I guess, but kind of panicked too. Which I guess he knew, which was why he was cutting off circulation to my arm.

I thought of my brother, asking me point-blank to come home, telling me he needed me, and I felt bad I could ignore him. I felt awful about my dad. I felt lousy about the no granddaughters and my mom's pain and how overwhelmed Bill was, but I couldn't go to them even if Bill came himself and got down on his knees.

I don't know why I could ignore that but could have Travis say *don't leave* and I wasn't going to go.

I turned into his arms, and I kissed him. I slid my body against his, and when the kiss turned deep and made me dizzy, I lifted my knee and wrapped my leg around him, hugging him close and opening myself at the same time. I grabbed his hand and moved it over my hip, toward my crease. I knew there would be no fucking now because we were too tired, but I needed to let him know he already had me, that I wasn't going. I needed to remind him I let him into me in ways I didn't let anybody else. I needed him to feel this was his body as much as mine. I needed him to know I understood this was more than I'd been pretending. That though it scared me, I was holding on.

I needed him to know I was glad he'd been there to catch me when I fell apart, glad he fought me when I told him I didn't want to be caught.

DINNER THE NEXT day was good. It wasn't quite as joyous as it would have been if I hadn't had the letter, and Haley asked me several times what was wrong. But Travis told her to let it go, and she did.

The turkey was not bad. Everybody seemed to enjoy the meal, and I was glad I didn't let Travis cancel it. I wished I hadn't felt so disconnected, wished I hadn't kept thinking about the Thanksgiving my family was having in Iowa.

That night we had the first snow of the year. Once everyone was gone and the dishes were cleaned up, Travis and I sat in the hot tub, wrapped in each other's arms, and watched it fall.

I was going to have to answer the letter eventually, I knew. I couldn't go home, but I couldn't not say anything, not when I knew what it had cost Bill to write. But I wasn't going to write him yet.

I leaned on Travis's shoulder. I felt the warmth of his body, the protective circle of his arms around me as we sat in silence and stillness and steam, and I felt okay again.

11

IT WAS RIGHT before Christmas when we got the dogs.

I went round and round with Travis about dogs for the operation. I pointed out we'd have an easier time herding and they could be an extra line of defense against predators, and when we needed to do a quick roundup for emergencies, we wouldn't have to call in as many hands. I sure could have used them for the calving. I even did the research with Haley's help on local border collie breeders who had cow dogs for sale.

Travis, as usual, put all his faith in his fence. Which, I had to admit, was good fence when it worked. Truth was, I wanted the dogs for the sheep, but I kind of wanted them for myself too. We always had dogs at the farm, and they were usually more than a little bit mine. One of them ran off trying to find me when I left. Obviously I hadn't had a dog since then, with all my traveling.

But Travis didn't want the fuss of puppies. He

pointed out border collies were hard to train and he'd have to get on some damned long list to get them and pay through the nose for the privilege of having to do all the work to train them. He was right.

It's just I really did want a dog.

Tory had a sweetheart of a pup, an ungodly mutt in at least ten directions, I swear. Polly was a brown-and-white-patched little lover whose main gene pool seemed to be terrier, and she always came up and gave me kisses when I stopped by the house. Having a good kitchen and people to feed inspired me, especially with Christmas coming on, and Travis made me farm the food out so he didn't get fat. I tried to tell him he could get off Chaucer and walk a bit more and eat what he liked, but that only got him cranky, so I started taking things over to Tory's place. It wasn't long before I kept a bag of dog biscuits in my car so I could slip a few to Polly when I came by.

I wasn't going to make a big deal out of it, and I did my best to keep my yen for a dog to myself. I was having plenty of fun on my own. We did up a tree too, just a small thing we cut down from the north pasture.

Travis didn't get out of his office much, but he did love his spread, enjoyed running it. I could never keep all that in my head the way he could. I need to get my hands in it, as Haley says. But Travis actually doesn't do well in real time. Which is why we don't make a bad team, in my opinion.

Ranching, I mean.

Anyway, we were doing up the holidays like nothing else. Cookies, cakes, stews and roasts, and twinkly lights in the windows. Haley got into it too, bringing over these big gaudy red plastic bows to hang on the stall doors, and I admit, they looked nice, though the horses sure didn't care. Travis took me on a lot of what Haley teased me were "romantic rides". In theory we were checking his precious fence, but mostly, yeah, we were just taking a nice ride. He was always on Chaucer, of course, and I ended up on Pepys.

It took me three weeks to figure out his name was not spelled "Peeps". It turns out Pepys was some old diary writer who fiddled under his maid's skirts. Chaucer had rung bells too, so I Googled. Apparently he wrote some important classic in Middle English. Travis said he was sometimes a little rude too.

"I thought you were a math guy, not a story guy," I said.

He shrugged. "Riley was an English major. His horse was Rochester." A smile flickered on his lips. "Riley liked to find the naughty bits in literature."

I didn't care much for that smile, but I told myself to get over it. "You miss him? Riley?"

Now the smile flashed at me, for me, and the sore spot in my midsection eased. "Not lately, no. I'm content to be the chatty one for a change."

He found it funny that I said he was chatty. But goddamn, he was.

Anyway. I was telling about the dogs.

I'd resigned myself to not having one. In fact, I reasoned, it was better. Because despite Travis's telling me he wanted me to stay, I wasn't some dummy thinking nothing was ever going to come between us. Something would. We were in a relationship. But lots of things could tear it apart, and eventually one of them would succeed. It'd be hard enough not to be with Travis, and the thought had driven me to braid many, many leathers. I surely didn't need to be missing a dog too.

But then one night when Haley and I were working, Travis stuck his head into the kitchen and told me we were getting up early in the morning and to get my ass to bed.

"Where are you going?" Haley asked, covering a yawn as she packed up her computer.

"I don't rightly know." I watched a second yawn follow, bigger than the first, and I frowned at her. "Listen, if coming over is making you tired—"

She waved a hand at me and shook her head. "It's these classes killing me. That and the cold. At least it's not supposed to snow again tomorrow." When she rose, she bent over and kissed me on the top of the head. "You two be safe wherever you go, okay?"

Haley was always kissing me on the top of the head. It was ridiculous how much I liked it. "Will do," I said.

I headed upstairs, where I knew Travis waited for me. Haley wouldn't have known what the extra little growl in his voice had been about when he told me it was time to go to bed, but I did. Before I headed to the bedroom, though, I hit the bathroom at the top of the stairs, did some business and some prep, and headed down the hall to meet him.

As I knew he would be, he was on the bed, lounging, wearing nothing but a pair of boxers. He doesn't look particularly hairy when he's dressed since he shaves close and generally wears long sleeves, but he's actually more than a bit of a bear. His gray-brown hair curls in a thick pelt across his chest and down his arms, and right then it caught the dim lamplight and made me want to jump onto the bed and bury my face in it. His right hand was tucked casually under the pillow, but it just thrilled me more. I knew why he was hiding it, knew what he was wearing there. He hid it to ramp me up.

I undressed without being asked, but I did it slow and extra clumsy, letting my eagerness and my nerves show, because I knew it ramped *him* up. But I was nervous, yeah. I saw the canister on the nightstand, and I saw the towel draped over the bed.

When I was naked, I went over to lie down on the towel. I pulled my legs open and waited.

He took his hand—cased in a glove—out from its hiding place and reached for the grease.

It turned me on when we did this all silent, no questions, no instructions, just looks and sounds, but it freaked me out too. For him it added to the wickedness of it all, that he was greasing up with Crisco to shove his fingers way up my ass. I lay there, still and quiet, staring into his eyes as he worked the first finger into me. He watched my face for the first few thrusts, but pretty soon he turned his attention to my ass.

It was fucking hot. He'd propped up a few pillows behind my head, but I leaned forward as much as I could to see his slicked-up fingers—two now—going inside me.

"We really are leaving early in the morning." He kept his eyes on his work, speaking casually, like working his fingers in and out of my ass was just something he had to get done before he went to bed. It made my blood hum.

"Where we headed?" I wasn't able to be casual. My voice was thick, and my words were raspy.

He added a third finger, and I moaned.

"East." He pushed in deep and twisted his fingers. "Going to check on something to see if it will work out."

That was all the information I was going to get about our errand tomorrow.

His pinky worked its way in beside the others, and I gave up, lay back and sang.

He had not properly fisted me yet, but the mindfuck was that he could have, because my body and mind were both ready. I was so fucking ready it wasn't funny. This game would end tonight, I knew, as it always did, with me red-faced and straining, looking up at him in a haze as I begged in slurred speech for him to please put his hand inside me and fuck me.

I would tell him how much I loved his fingers scraping inside me. I would describe my insides with crude and ridiculous terms both, knowing he liked it. Why the hell he got turned on by me saying I wanted him to stroke my velvet channel I don't rightly know, but Jesus did that make him bite hard on my lip. I wanted so bad to look down and just see his wrist or forearm showing. I wanted to know he was in me. I wanted to feel so vulnerable and safe at once. I wanted it as I had never wanted anything else.

He greased his hand like you would not believe, working each one of the fingers inside me, pairing them, dividing them, teasing them. Two days before, he had me over the couch while we watched a porn where two guys interrogated a prisoner who had allegedly smuggled film canisters in his ass. Travis wore surgical gloves, but in the video it had been a black glove.

That night Travis had just about climbed the walls. He dug around in my ass, biting my ear as he whispered, "You got anything in there I need to find?"

"Yeah. Get in there and get it." But he couldn't find it, he said, so he'd have to dig deeper, and pretty soon I was pleading and clenching, sure this was going to be the time he went all the way in. But no.

There was no way it was going to be tonight, with him telling me we had to get up in the morning. But the game was that I begged, so I did.

"What do you want, Roe?" He had his hand cupped, thumb tucked, four fingers pushed in to the first knuckle. I was so well greased you could have rammed a silage tower up my ass.

"I want your hand in my ass." I tried to fuck myself on his fingers. "I want to feel your fingers at the back of my throat. I want you to fuck me up to your elbow. I want you to tickle me from the inside. I want your big, bad hand punching at me, making me whine. I want you to fuck me with your fist, Mr. Loving."

It took me a bit to say all that. Speeches are tricky when you are acutely aware of your ass being stretched. If he'd get his hand *in*, it'd be a fucking relief. I'd be full as fuck, but the pain would ease. But then his fun of torturing me would end. It was my job to take what he dished out, so I told him what I wanted, then got ready not to get it.

That night he leaned over me, looked at me with wicked, wicked eyes, and said, "You remember, boy. I always give you want you want."

He pushed inside.

To say I screamed would make it sound a lot more like a little girl than was right to describe a man sticking his hand up another man's ass. The sound started at the base of my spine and came out the top of my head instead of my mouth. I will not lie to you. There was a moment of pretty significant pain. But it wasn't tearing or anything dangerous. Just stretching. My body opening to take Travis inside where he wanted to go.

Then he was in.

In. Inside me. I could feel him. It was alarming and

arousing at once. He was some kind of beautiful, terrible invader. I was very aware of my internal organs. It felt like I'd taken a demon in me, that all he had to do was open his hand, bare his claws and snatch parts of me away.

I'd waited months for this, aching for the moment I could see what it looked like to have his hand up me, but now that it was here, all I could do was stare at his face, caught as I had never been caught before.

He held my gaze.

He turned his hand.

My cry was a moan this time. When he started to thrust, it was as if I were back in Iowa with the hogs. All I could do was grunt, grunt, grunt, then moan-grunt again when he turned his hand. Oh, he *loved* turning his hand.

I loved and feared this. So *dangerous*.

I *loved* it.

This wasn't some game. This was huge, what I let him do to me. This was more than letting him at a few inches of my rectum. He was *in me*. This was more trust than I knew I had in me to give.

I realized why I couldn't turn away, because I could see he knew all this too. He got what a big deal this was. When I looked at him, I knew he was going to take good care of me.

He pushed in so deep my eyes watered, and I licked my lips before opening them.

Go in me here too.

He did.

We kissed like drunken fools while he plunged his fist in and out of me. That actually gives the wrong impression of what happened—fingers always go in first, but the image in my head is of his hand pounding at me. Of his arm going deep inside me. Of my being so open after the first few thrusts, he just slipped in.

We had watched more fisting videos than I could count. Travis's favorite was this one where some guy all tricked out in leather and spikes rammed his fist deep inside this guy bent over on a bench, punching with these quick thrusts before he—and here I always started to twitch and squirm—pulled one hand out and shoved the other one in, then alternated hands thrust for thrust. They showed him putting on a lot of lube, but I'm here to tell you it takes more than what they showed for the easy stuff.

I thought of that guy and his ass-reaming as Travis's tongue tangled around mine and his hand moved seamlessly in and out of me, still dangerous, but so in tune with me I could feel it. My whole body gave over to him. My body trusted him, not just my mind. Trusted him with everything.

He had never done this before with anybody. He had only done this with me. It was selfish as hell, but I wanted so badly for me to always be the only one. No matter what happened I'd be the man who first let him in this deep.

I could have gone all night, but he only gave me a

few minutes, which was smart, but it made me crazy nuts. I attacked him when he withdrew. I slurred and begged, telling him I needed more fucking, that I was a slut, Mr. Loving, and I needed some fucking now. *Please fuck me, Mr. Loving.*

The next thing I knew, his cock was buried in my throat. He straddled my head, grabbed my hair and fucked my mouth, and I took it like a greedy bastard, jacking off the whole time. I felt dirty and raw and wonderful, and when he came all over my face, I grinned and opened wide, shutting my eyes because he went fucking everywhere on me while I shot too. It was great.

He was really gentle with me after, cleaning me up head to toe in the bathroom, and grilling me like a mother hen about the state of my ass.

"I'm fine," I told him for the fiftieth time. "Sore, yeah, but fine. Abso-fucking-lutely fine."

He kissed me and stroked my ass cheek. "You were so beautiful. I shouldn't have done it because we do need to get up early. But I couldn't resist anymore." Another kiss, this one deeper. "Thank you."

We made out for a while, but he didn't let it go on too long, herding me to the bed instead. Though he did spoon up against my back and play with my nipples a little. This was the other part of our game, and fisting apparently wasn't going to make us skip it.

"I wish we could do it every fucking night." I shifted so he could get better access to my chest. I knew he wanted to rile me up good before telling me I had to get to sleep, and I wanted it too. I had the craziest dreams when he did that to me.

He nuzzled my neck and pinched my nipple hard enough to make me gasp. "I'd like to keep you in a cage, legs tied open, ass strapped to a hole where I could come by and finger-fuck you any damn time I wanted to."

I shivered. This was a newer game, where he turned into some sort of raunchy dungeon master and explained in graphic detail the ways he would enslave me. He said shit I knew he would never, ever do, but it really turned him on to say it to me. This sort of rough talk, where it wasn't just about sex but about me one step above a dog was not something I generally went in for, but when Travis said it, it sounded pretty good.

"Yeah?" I said.

"Yeah. I might let you out sometimes to bend you over my desk. You could hold yourself open for me and give me a nice view."

Okay, that made me squirm. "Mmm."

He pinched hard again. "But where you'd look nicest is on a bench, your ass red and pointing in the air. I'd strap your ankles and wrists, and I'd make a day of your ass. You look so good with tails. But now that I know how much you like big things in your ass, we might have to make some changes. Bigger tails at least. And other things. I've shown you those videos. You need a thick gag in your mouth too. I don't want to hear you fuss when I do all this to you. I just want to hear the slap of my hand on your ass and the slick of my arm going deep into you."

Oh fuck, but I was whimpering and writhing against him now, and I was hard. Really fucking hard, though my sore ass had sworn it wasn't possible.

Which is of course why he slid his hand down to my hip and patted it smartly. "Time to go to sleep."

It took me almost an hour, and I dreamed I was tied up and passed around between seven sexy men who did nothing but finger my ass. That part of my anatomy was still sore in the morning when he woke me, but between the dream and everything he'd done to me the night before, I got off in the shower by touching myself twice.

We'd done it. We'd actually done it. I felt like a deflowered virgin, though technically it was my second time fisting. I didn't care. I felt pretty fucking awesome. Whatever the hell we were doing "east", it couldn't be better than what we'd done the night before.

I was so wrong.

WE ATE ON the fly and took coffee to go, and then we went halfway across the state to a cozy little farm down a gravel road. It was a border collie rescue.

Dogs. He was getting me two dogs.

I didn't know what to say, so I stared up at him. We were out at the kennels, and it was cold, and my ears were going numb underneath the hat he'd bought me for my birthday. His cheeks were pink as he grinned at me.

"Oh, don't look so shocked. I knew you wanted dogs."

Despite the cold, my face flushed with heat. "But you said *you* didn't want them."

"I said I didn't want to fuss with them. But you do. So they're yours. Go check them all out and see if there are any you want to work with. We can do pups if you'd rather, but I thought maybe you'd want to see the rescue first."

That last bit got to me in ways I hadn't anticipated. It was true, it'd be better to get pups from a litter, to know the parents and have them be stable, solid work dogs. But those were hard to find and expensive. All these dogs were ones owners had abandoned, and few of them had been ranch dogs. Their owners had thought border collies would be cute and fun and had no idea how much work they were getting into. They were also frequently border collies with a bit of mutt in them. In short, they were a mess.

I ended up with a pair of two-year-olds named Ezra and Ezekiel, but I was already shortening them to Ez and Zeke while Travis wrote the check. I liked the shorter names because they'd be easy to bark out while we were working. And I meant these boys to work. They'd been out at somebody's acreage, presents for two little girls, but they were too rambunctious. The owners had meant well, but these dogs were more stir-crazy than most of their breed, and they needed some work to calm them the hell down. Trouble was, no ranch or farm wanted them because they were going to take too much time to train and might never come completely up to snuff.

They *were* handfuls. Just getting them to Nowhere was work enough. We had to stop three times to let them run, and in the end the only way they didn't drive Travis nuts was for me to sit in the back mini-seat with them. This is his truck, mind you, so there I am with my legs sprawled, one of them angled up onto the front seat while two dogs climbed all over me wanting to tell me how much they liked me. After I accepted kisses for about an hour, they finally settled down, one on my chest and one across my groin, and they napped.

I must have too, because the next thing I knew, Travis was stroking my thigh, and we were closing in on the lane to the ranch.

It took me the better part of a month to get them to come to any kind of heel, and they were never going to win any championships. They were lucky to remember where their food dish was most days. But Ez and Zeke are good dogs, and they mind me enough to get the job done. I love coming home and seeing them bound down the lane.

THE DOGS WERE with us on Christmas morning, impatient because for reasons they couldn't understand I wasn't giving them any work, and to make matters worse, Tory and his family were coming over. Before people arrived I took the boys out to give them a good run.

When I got back, Haley stood on the porch steps, eyes red and shoulders hunched.

I don't know how I knew before she said it. All I can tell you is when she opened her mouth and said on a sob, "I'm pregnant," I wasn't surprised. I was just sorry I'd been right.

12

THOUGH HALEY HAD scared me at first, she's actually one of the sweetest, nicest girls I've ever met. She's also just about the toughest, and I know it sounds messed up to say she is sweet and tough, but she manages it. Haley lures you into a soft place with her sweetness and keeps you out of trouble by being tough and stubborn.

For the first time since ever, I had a friend, and Haley was it. Her dad was the best manager I'd ever worked for, and obviously I was intimate as all hell with Travis, but Haley was an actual friend. She was somebody I could laugh with or do things with and, yeah, sometimes even talk with. She talked a hell of a lot more than me. But every now and again I told her things too.

A few weeks before Christmas, I'd told her about the letters from home.

I hadn't planned to. It just sort of came out one night while Travis was riding and we were doing GED prep at the kitchen table. She was trying to explain essays to me, which made me think of the letter, and then damned if I wasn't dumping all my dirty laundry all over. I did it in about six sentences, but it was more than I ever expected to give, and I think for half a minute we both sat there too shocked to move.

Eventually she asked questions, and I answered them, and that went on until I'd given her most of the sordid story. She knew about me getting kicked out. She knew about prison. She knew about Kayla and my parents both being sick and Bill's blank shots. I told her, too, that I didn't think I could go back, sure she was going to hate me.

She didn't. She was pissed off, but not at me. In fact, she launched a stream of cussing at my family and my brother, and I decided then and there it would be best she never met Kayla, because one of them was going to get arrested. I honestly don't quite understand most of what she said. Haley gets philosophical a lot, and most of it went over my head. She carried on about how they were happy to tell me about their lives but had absolutely no interest in mine.

I had felt comfortable with Haley before, but she felt like an old glove after that night. She taught me the GED stuff, but after that was done, she hung around so we could chat. She told me about her favorite music. She could sit for hours and go on and on about the poetry of the lyrics, and I swear to God, there were some songs she played for me where a certain note would hit and she would start to cry. It was nice music. Haley made me a CD of her favorites, and I played it sometimes while I worked in the kitchen.

Haley never bossed, and when she told me I did a good job, she never patronized me. Haley is a real class act.

The night she told me she was pregnant, it cut me to the bone to see her so lost and scared.

It was fucking cold outside, twenty below with windchill, and here she was, pregnant, not even wearing a coat. I could tell by the way she looked I was the first she'd told. She wanted the two of us to go off and talk about it. I had no idea what in God's name I was going to say, but I figured mostly she needed to talk and to cry.

I will tell you, I was damn scared. But this was Haley. I had to do it.

I took my coat off, bussed a kiss on her cheek and squeezed her shoulder. "You go on up to my apartment over the barn. Turn the heat up as high as you want. Let me tell Travis where we're headed so people don't fuss, and I'll be up."

She nodded, wiping her eyes on my coat sleeve. She seemed like she wanted a hug, and I wanted to give her one, but I was mindful of the cold and gave her another gentle but firm, "Go on," and she got.

I relaxed as I saw Ez and Zeke catch up with her and follow her to the stairs. It would be hard to be too down with those nuts trying to cover her in slobber.

Travis was already hunting for me, and I met him in the hall by his office. "I need to go sit with Haley a bit. I sent her to my apartment."

That made him frown, but it was because I'd said *my*. His latest thing was to ask me why the hell I had to keep stuff over there when there was so much space at the house. I had my reasons, but I wasn't going to get into it now.

"She's in trouble." I kept my voice low, but as soon as I said the words, I knew they were the wrong ones. He was about to tell me how her dad and mom deserved to know if there was trouble, and before I knew what I was doing, I blurted, "She's pregnant."

I felt bad telling him, because I knew Haley wanted it secret, but it felt good to tell him too. Everything got easier as soon as I got it off my chest.

He looked tired and sad. "Shit. What's she going to do?"

"I don't know. I figure that's what we're gonna talk about." Then all of a sudden the nerves came back, and I reached for his hand. "I'm scared I'm going to say the wrong thing."

His fingers stroked mine, and he gave me a one-sided smile. "Just listen mostly, I would say, and be kind. She's probably beat herself up plenty on her own."

I nodded and brushed a kiss on his mouth in silent thanks. He caught my chin and kissed me again, a lingering, sweet one.

I carried it with me across the yard all the way to the

barn.

Halfway over I backtracked and went to my car to get a CD. It was one of the artists she'd played for me, and I listen to it while I drive around. I brought it along to play while we talked.

She laughed and smiled and asked if I went and bought this on my own, which of course I had, which made her all the happier. I put it in the player and turned it down soft and got her a soda from the mini fridge. I got myself a beer. I had the feeling I was going to need it.

I sat her on my bed, and I perched on the arm of the saggy chair by the TV with the dogs at my feet. I settled in to listen.

She stared at the carpet a lot while she talked, which wasn't like her at all.

"It's Cal's." She grimaced. "But since he accused me of sleeping around, he's never going to believe he's the father. Anyway, I don't want him messed up in this. I don't want a thing from him. He doesn't know, and he's not going to." Her voice broke on the end, and she sighed and wiped at her eyes with her fingers. "Sorry."

Being in the chair felt safe, but I could tell for her I was too far away. I rose, stepped over the dogs and sat hesitantly beside her. She melted against my side, crying softly as she went on.

"Roe, I'm so scared. This is going to ruin my whole life. My *whole life*. No school now. Aren't I an awful mother already, that this is all I can think about?" She laughed, but it had jagged edges. "Want to know the worst of all? I keep hoping I'll miscarry and not have to worry about it. I'm so awful."

That went right up my nose. "Hey. You aren't awful." A gear turning since she'd told me on the steps clicked into place. "Are you…I mean, are you going to…get rid of it?"

This time the laugh was so bitter it made me jump. "Abortion, you mean. I tried. I went yesterday. On Christmas Eve, I went to kill my baby."

"Don't say it like that," I shot back, sharper than I meant. But I couldn't seem to gentle either. This was a rough conversation all around. "And what do you mean, you went yesterday? Your mom take you? She knows?"

"I went by myself."

I was so mad I had to stand up because I was shaking, and my hands were balling into fists. The dogs sat up too, and they started barking. "You went to get an abortion *by yourself?* What the hell, Haley? You just drove—what, to Rapid City?"

"Scottsbluff. I remember about the law they passed in South Dakota about abortion. They repealed it, but I didn't know if there'd be pickets. I went to a women's center. I'm three months along." She hung her head. "I couldn't do it. I couldn't go through with it. There weren't even any protesters, but I couldn't do it. I think actually I could have done it if they *had* been there. I'd have been angry at them for telling me what I can and can't do to my body. But there wasn't anybody. Just nice, polite staff who were very understanding. And I couldn't go through with it. I couldn't—"

She broke off, choked on a sob and drew her knees up to her chest. "I wasn't thinking about little toes or hands. I wasn't feeling guilty. I just—couldn't."

I put a tentative arm around her. She cried for a while. Ez and Zeke rested their heads on my knees and whined.

When she seemed to wind down a bit, I said, "Like you said. It's come up fast on you."

"I'm not stupid. We used condoms. I swear we did. But then I was late, and…I don't know. I had this feeling. I thought I was being silly. But I took three tests, three different kinds. And they were all positive." She gave a ragged sigh against my sleeve. "I'm due June ninth."

That seemed a long time away, and yet it was not very far at all. "Take a while to think it over, and if you decide you want an abortion, I'll take you to a place without any damn protesters. You shouldn't have to see that shit." I tried to remember if Iowa had made any laws like that. I wanted to believe it hadn't, but I really didn't know. It hadn't been something I cared about. Not until now.

I thought of how passionately Haley defended gay rights without anybody asking her to, and I felt pretty low.

"I will take you all the way to Canada if I have to," I told her.

She hugged me tight, then sat up wearily. "I don't know if I want to have one. I mean, there are a lot of nice people who want to adopt, and babies are hard to find. Just look at your brother. Well…I mean, no offense, but I'm not giving my baby to somebody who thinks your orientation needs to be healed. I might not give it to anybody. I don't know. What I do know is I want to think about it."

She teared up. "No matter what I do, everything is ruined. Even if I do get an abortion, I'm not a dipshit bitch who can go get an abortion like it's a manicure—which is what the protesters seem to think. I bet you my student loan check the same 'good Christians' who would call me a baby killer would rather turn and shout at you for being gay before they'd take ten minutes to help me through this. They don't give a shit about anybody but themselves. If I keep my baby and ask for their help, the next thing they'll do is find something wrong with me. Fuck them and their *pro-life*." She had stopped crying in the middle of her rant, and now she glared across the room at the wall. "If I keep this baby, I'm going to make damn sure it grows up to kick their bigoted, hateful asses."

On the one hand part of me wanted to say she was being a little harsh, that probably some people really did mean well and would help her, because nobody could be nasty all the time. But a deeper part of me drowned the reasonable voice and said yes.

Yes, that's exactly it. You have to hate them back and shut them off so they don't hurt you. Things are already bad, and you can't, whatever you do, let them get any worse. You have to keep them out before they can make it bad.

Then there was a *third* me, watching both these conversations and getting confused, thinking something wasn't quite right, but the water was rising and Haley was crying again, and I just rode the waves and hoped like hell everything eventually settled down.

"Whatever you decide, Haley," I said, quiet but steady, "whatever you decide, I will help you if you want. I don't know a damn thing about babies, but I'll help you if you keep it. I'll just…" I lost some of my confidence and started to stammer as I said the rest. "You've been a good friend to me. Best I ever had. That Cal, he's a fucking dick and an idiot to leave a girl like you. If I were straight, I'd be on my fucking knees for you. I would be there for you and the baby. Even if it wasn't mine."

She burst into really bad tears then, and I felt like shit because I knew I'd fucked it up. My chest was so tight I had to work to breathe, and I was putting myself together enough to say sorry, when she threw her arms around my neck, squeezed me tight, and said, "I love you, Monroe Davis."

Something inside me broke open, and when I let the air out of my lungs, it was shaky. For the first time in a while I wanted to run, run like my heels were on fire.

Then I felt the wet of her tears on my neck, and the fire must have been there, because it went out. I wrapped my arms carefully around her and let my head rest against the side of her head. "Love you too, Haley."

There, on Christmas Day up in my apartment holding Haley while she cried with the dogs by us, that was when I had my first glimpse of home.

January 5

Dear Bill,

The first thing I want to tell you is I'm fine. I'm working as a senior hand at a place called Nowhere Ranch. It's a very nice spread, about three thousand acres. Most of it is grass, and this is western Nebraska, so it's not so much for farming. This is also kind of a hobby ranch. The owner keeps cattle and sheep, but only about five hundred head of each, though those numbers change every day, and Travis Loving does know his numbers. He used to teach math at college in Omaha.

He's had some trouble with the sheep, and there I think I'm pulling my weight. Who thought all those years of sheep at the old farm would come to some use? We even have some dogs. They are pieces of work, but you might remember I kind of have a way with dogs. They are coming around pretty good, I think.

Speaking of school. I'm actually working right now to take my GED. I'm going to take it online. A friend is helping me study. She is so smart you wouldn't believe it. She is going to be a great teacher. I'm kind of a test case for her. But she doesn't need practice. She's great already. I wish she had been my teacher. I think I would've done a lot better in school.

The other thing I need to tell you is I can't come back to the farm. I imagine that will sound hard to you, and I'm sorry. I am upset about Dad and about Mom, and I am real sorry about the babies. I do want to help you, and I'm sorry it's all falling to you same as always.

But the problem is I could tell from your letter you actually don't want me to come home. Not the me I am. That kind of sounds like hog shit, I know, but hear me out. I think this has been the problem since I was about ten. I think I knew then I was a Roe who wasn't what everybody wanted me to be. I tried as hard as I could to be that Roe, but it didn't work out no matter what I tried. There may be guys who can change who they are, but I'm not one of them. That might make you sad or angry. I know it was hell for me to swallow. But let me tell you angry and sad don't change it.

I can't come home because I'm still gay, and I know from Kayla's letter and yours this is a problem for you all. Which means I'm a problem for you all. Which means it would be best I don't come home.

I understand you will likely read this and figure me for a jerk who doesn't care about his family. From where I stand, if I'm a jerk, it's me being a jerk while knowing it would be a lot easier on everyone if I didn't come back and remind everybody so loudly I'm not who you want me to be. And to be honest, it isn't a whole lot of picnic to walk around having everyone tell you what you are is wrong.

The thing is neither you or Kayla asked me in your letters how I was. You acted like the best I could get was one step above the gutter. This is why I started this letter with a list of what I'm doing. Maybe I'm not as great as everybody else, but for me I'm doing okay. I don't know about healed. I suspect there is something wrong with me, maybe, but it ain't that I'm gay. What I do know is being here at Nowhere has made a lot of things right which used to feel real wrong.

I would love to come home and see Mom and Dad and you and to meet your wife. If it turns out I misread your letters and you're okay with me as I am, please tell me, and I will come home and apologize right to your face and help out in every way I can. If not, it's best nobody write me anymore. It sounds like the last thing you need is to be fighting with me over who I sleep with on top of everything else.

Please tell Mom I love her. I've been praying for her and for Dad too. I would have you tell Dad I love him too, but I will leave that up to you to relay or not. I don't want him upset.

I love you too, Bill. I miss you. Despite what you may think of me, I have always looked up to you and to Dad, and I've tried to be the kind of man the both of you could be proud of. Whether you decide to contact me or let sleeping dogs lie is a decision I will leave to you.

Love,
Roe

13

I HAVE BEEN through some shitty winters in my day. Nobody does shit winters like the Dakotas, except maybe Canada. But my first winter at Nowhere was the fucking worst I ever knew.

It was so cold we lost some livestock. We had shelters up for them, but it still got too cold, and any sick were gone. Some of them were pregnant ewes too, which bit double. If I wasn't out dragging heaters to water troughs—heaters which kept fucking breaking or shorting out—I was trying to rig up better shelters and haul more hay. It snowed all the fucking time, and when it didn't snow, it blew. Twice the power went out, and then in addition to dragging hay and heaters, we were hauling generators too.

Tory didn't have a generator, so we bundled his family up at our place. Two of the hands stayed with us too. They didn't have heat either, and their pipes were freezing. We were one hell of a pile there in Travis's half-empty house. Dogs too. We were all crammed in there.

Which was, actually, when it started to fill up with stuff.

I think Travis was waiting for me to decorate or something, which frankly pissed me off. Just because I like cooking doesn't mean I want to pick out curtains and shit. Besides, he had too much damn house for one man. Even two men. That was why I kept the apartment. I wasn't having any part of it.

Haley, however…

She was about five months along when we went through the no-power period. I should explain though we had a generator for the house and another for the ranch equipment, we were not cooking roasts and soaking in the hot tub. You only get so much juice from those generators, and you have to rotate things through. You can have the fridge, or you can have the furnace. You can have hot water, or you can run the washing machine. When shit goes down in the field and the generator out there gets kicked over by a pissed-off cow, you unplug the one at the house and use it for the livestock while you fix the broken one and hope for the best, and in the meantime you use a lot of blankets.

Enter Haley.

Here we were busting ass to keep the stock alive and all piled in on top of each other, turning into popsicles and getting really fucking tired of cold meat sandwiches or grilling in a blizzard, and tripping over the dogs, and Haley decided what we really ought to be doing was furnishing Travis's damn house. At first we thought she was joking, and boy did that go down bad. She said no, damn it, we were going to fix his place right now.

We had all been kind of treading on eggshells around Haley, and though this was fucking nuts, this "let's redecorate in a blizzard," nobody wanted to be the one to point it out. Her parents were amazingly cool about the pregnancy thing. Well, Tory did try to punch out Cal. And from what I gather, there was a lot of crying and arguing and hugging and more crying between all of them.

Then pretty much they faced it. Haley was still in school, but nobody knew about the summer or fall. She was going back and forth between giving the baby—a girl, according to the last ultrasound—up for adoption and keeping it. Her mom had said she would help, but the trouble was Haley had to go away to go to school. There was no education program around close enough for her to commute. So her mom would have to watch the kid for a few years, or Haley would have to have daycare wherever she went, which would cost them something dear.

But the adoption thing had hiccups too. Haley was dead set it had to be the right family, and she didn't like any of them she saw in the files. I wondered privately if any of them were my brother and his wife. I mean, what the hell were the odds, but it made me think. Seemed so weird, my brother aching for a baby, Mom wanting a granddaughter and here was Haley looking for a good home for her baby girl.

It bothered me my family wasn't a good home. It bothered me that Haley was right. Admitting it made me feel hollow and sad and confused.

Everybody tried to do their best to give Haley a break, to let her snap and crab and sometimes cry, and so we helped redecorate Travis's house because it was what she wanted.

To a point it was practical. We were sleeping in piles. Travis and I had his bed, Haley and her mom had the spare, Tory took the pull-out couch, and the hands and Haley's brother had the empty rooms. They'd dragged my bed down and over from the apartment after a few days of sleeping on the floor. We'd go a week without power, we'd get it back for two days, and then another storm would take it out for three weeks. It was on the national news, it was so bad. There had never been a rural outage quite like this. Livestock were dying left and right. All of us were scared to death some fool ewe would decide this would be a fine time to go into labor and really show us the meaning of hell.

There wasn't much for it though but shore up and wait and hope. We could use something to do, and we could use better decor and somewhere to sleep. We got it from all over. Walmart. The barn. My apartment. The Parrish house. Some of it came from the hands' places and even some from Goodwill.

She painted too. We covered the bare white walls in colored paint Haley found here, there and everywhere.

Obviously we did the painting, but she gave the direction. You know, it kept our mind off things. And once there was actually some furniture and stuff on the walls, it was a little easier to sit there under blankets and pretend we weren't freezing our asses off. It got just a tiny bit better. So maybe Haley wasn't so nuts.

In the kitchen Haley hung these brass molds around the rim above the cupboards, things from her family's attic. She did this cool stuff with old tack too. Wrapped horseshoes and leather leads and stuff you would have thought was junk, old cans and such, and yet when she was done, it was pretty fucking amazing.

The dining rooms and living rooms were the best. We had already set up card tables and lawn chairs in the dining room so we could eat, but Haley dragged decorations from her high school graduation over, and when she got done, it looked as if we were going to have a luau or something. She had patio lights on a string, which I thought would be for show since we couldn't turn them on, but no, they had batteries. She cut out a palm tree from boxes and painted it too. Then there were the umbrellas. They looked like the kind you'd stick in a drink, but they were bigger. We ate by battery string light and candlelight in a fake Hawaiian getaway. It was actually kind of fun.

In the living room there was a funky braided rug in front of the fire with four chairs around it. One from the four-season room, the recliner, one from Goodwill, and one from my apartment. The spare bedroom was

Paul and Aaron's place now. Aaron was another one of the hands. They had brought over half their stuff outside of furniture, though they'd brought some of that too, small stuff to hold clothes and things, and they seemed to enjoy being here. Once I heard them whispering maybe this spring they could jockey for my apartment, since I wasn't using it. I will tell you I didn't care much for that, but I know I was being petty. I wasn't using it. And Travis was talking about expanding. He would do better to have hands on site besides me.

Honestly, after Haley's decoration-hunt gutting, there wasn't much left up there. I had already brought over my leather stuff because I worked it at night before bed. I played cards and carried on with everybody for a while, and then I went upstairs and braided until Travis came to bed. The idea of moving out of the apartment for good made me nervous, but I supposed it was time to start thinking about it.

We were all so stressed out, and we so wanted our full electricity back, but the funny thing is, when it came on again, I was almost sad. For one day it was amazing and great. We filled the hot tub up, turned on every light in the house, and I cooked like it was Christmas. We watched TV, and one of the hands had a Wii, so we hooked it up and played it. It was kind of fun. I ended up later buying one myself. Bowling in my living room. What a world.

But after everyone had showered with as much hot water as they wanted and had eaten and relaxed, they went home. For somebody who worked hard not to have friends or engage in conversation, I had gotten awful attached to everybody being around all the time. I mean, here I could finally cook for people, and now nobody was home.

I never said anything about feeling down, but Travis seemed to figure it out. He was especially tender those first few days. He never said a word about it, just noticed and gave me extra petting.

It was a long, hard winter. But it's still one of my favorite memories.

I MENTIONED I'D been braiding leather in bed. There's a story about that too.

Once I gave the leather bracelet to Haley, other people started to notice it, and when she told them I made it for her, they asked me if I had others. One woman in town tried to pay me to make her one. It upset me for a few days because she didn't take *no* very well, and I started doing my shopping really early in the morning or asking Travis or Haley to pick things up for me so I didn't run into her.

Part of the problem is I put extra into the bracelet for Haley. It looked too crude for her when I was done, so I undid it, and this time I wove some metal beads into it. Then it looked too heavy. I made it half as wide as I usually do, and I staggered the silver beads evenly around it. It was on brown leather, and I worried it should have been black, but Haley said it was perfect and to stop fussing. And she wore it every day.

I gave the extras to her and asked if she knew someone somewhere who would want them. Do you know what she did? She gave them to everybody. Her mom, her dad—Tory even wore his sometimes when he went into town. Her mom's was a necklace cord, and she put some pendant on it.

You get one guess as to who didn't get one and got uppity.

How was I supposed to know Travis would get bent out of shape? I figured they were junk to keep my hands busy, but suddenly they were a hot commodity. I didn't like it. I stopped letting anyone have them. Some I threw away. But it was already too late. Travis had seen them, and now he saw me fussing with them when I went to bed.

"They're just these things I do with my hands," I told him. "They aren't anything really."

"The one you made for Haley is very nice. Everybody says so. The others are nice too. Everybody who wears them gets comments about them."

Meaning they weren't commenting about his because he didn't have one.

Okay. So I understood they meant things to other people, and I knew Travis wanted one. But I couldn't give him one of the pieces of garbage I would have given to Goodwill. You saw how I fussed over Haley's. I wouldn't have given it to her at all, except she hounded me. There was no way I was ever going to be able to make one good enough for Travis.

I did try. I tried so many different things. I had been trying since the middle of December, thinking I would give him something for Christmas, but nothing worked, and anyway it seemed dumb the more I thought about it.

By February I had a boxful of things I'd tried to make for Travis and given up on. The best was a belt. I looked it up on the Internet and bought one of somebody else's and tore it apart to see how to do it right. But when I was done it seemed so crude, like a kid had made it. I put it away.

I tried a bracelet, but the first one was too fat, the second too thin. I tried putting bits of metal on one. Not beads. I actually picked up odd bobs and nuts and things from all over the ranch, thinking he'd like how Nowhere was in it. I really thought that one was going to work. But in the end it looked as dumb as everything else. I tried a circlet too, for his neck. I fashioned the NR brand out of wire and hung it from the center. But it was as bad as everything else, and I gave up.

Well, sometimes I tried little things. But I stopped pretending I was going to give them to him.

Then one weekend Travis found the box.

We'd been busy all week gearing up for lambing. Nowhere does calving in the fall, which is smart for so many reasons, but the smartest is in the spring we can focus on lambing and then shearing. There's all sorts of stuff about timing and nutrition, and Travis had caved finally, and we were vaccinating some and giving antibiotics. All this had been turned ass-over-teakettle with the storms and the outage, and so there was a lot to set to rights. But once we had it mostly together, Travis declared we were going to have a quiet evening at home. Which for him was code that I would make us a nice dinner, he'd pour alcohol into me until I was really loose, and then we'd fuck like bunnies. Worked for me.

I fixed sirloin tips in gravy with some nice vegetables and bread, and mashed potatoes with a little bit of sour cream and garlic in them. It was pretty good if I do say so. I was cutting into a blueberry pie and debating adding ice cream when Travis came into the kitchen. He was holding the box of the stuff I had made for him.

He was really pissed off.

I was too. I put down the pie knife and stalked over, heart pounding, and I tried to take the box from him. "That ain't yours."

He pulled it out of my reach. "Oh, isn't it?" He held up the bracelet with his initials woven in with beads, and I winced. He threw it into the box. "What is this, Roe? And don't give me any shit about waiting for a special occasion. My birthday was in February. You gave me a bottle of wine and a blowjob."

I felt like he'd slapped me, except as soon as the hurt hit, guilt washed it over. Okay, so I'd given him a bad gift. "The stores were closed because of the storm."

He rattled the box in my face. "Made all this between now and then, did you?"

"It's *shit*." My hands were shaking, and my stomach hurt so much I wanted to double over. "It's all crap, okay? I tried, but they all turned out shit. Same as everything else I do, all right?"

"There's nothing wrong with any of this. This is *better* than the one you made for Haley, and they're still talking about it in the Women's Circle." He slammed the box on the counter and glared at me. "You put all that time into the bracelet for Haley, and she wears it everywhere. You gave one to everyone but me, and everybody knows it. It's great gossip. 'Oh, they're living together, but it must not be serious.' They're saying that. They really are."

"Because I didn't give you some stupid leather-braided piece of shit?"

"Because you treat me like your boss and your fuck buddy!"

"Well, you are!"

The words, bellowed from my gut, hung like cannonballs in the air. Or bombs, maybe. When we let them land, they were going to explode.

Except Travis spoke so softly it cut under my shouting. "That all I am, Roe?"

I got mad. I got so mad, but I couldn't let it out, which made me madder. *All he was.* He figured I moved in with just anybody? Had he missed the part where I said I really didn't fuck anybody twice? Had he slept through my telling him about my family and why I was out here instead of back home? Had he not been paying any fucking attention to anything I did in the now-almost-year I'd been here?

I was confused. I was scared. I was nervous, afraid I had fucked this up, but I couldn't tell how. It was a bad fight, and we weren't even yelling.

In my head I was back in Algona, my dad had those magazines in his hand, my mom was crying, and all I could think was it was going to end. I would lose Haley and the baby and Tory and the dogs and the damn sheep.

And Travis.

I shoved the box at him, chest tight and vision blurry. "Go on then. Go on and take whatever the fuck you want. You want that garbage, you can have it. I never *gave* it to anybody else. They just took it or got it from Haley, and I only gave her the one because she wouldn't shut up. It's all crap too. All of it, everything." I picked up the pie, and I tossed the whole thing into the sink. "It's all *shit*. Shit, shit, shit, and if you want it, you can fucking have it, but when it's crap, I don't want to hear about it, because *I told you that was what it was.*"

My chest and stomach hurt so bad now I knew I was in trouble, so I stormed out of the kitchen, and then because I knew there wasn't going to be anywhere I could get away from him inside, I kept going out the front door. No coat. I ain't an idiot, though. I grabbed my boots and stuffed my feet into them as I went down the steps.

For a second I thought about heading to my apartment, but he'd come after me there. Anyway, there wasn't anything there hardly. Not even a scrap of leather.

Not that I would ever be able to work a fucking leather ever again.

I shouted and slammed at gates, pushing deeper and deeper into the ranch. Past the barn, out into the pens we had sorted the pregnant ewes into. I didn't even check on them. I just kept going. There was this whisper gnawing on me, asking me where the fuck I thought I was going, but that made my chest tighter, and I shook my head, clenched my teeth and whispered, "Nowhere. I ain't going nowhere."

Then I realized I was already there. I was such shit I fucked up nowhere.

I started to run. I ran past the sheep, past the horses, toward the cattle wintering pasture. Past the road Travis took for his rides and headed out into the hayfields. I had no fucking plan and no coat and nowhere to go, so I just ran. I ran from the past and from the pain I had set myself up for the second I'd walked into that bar in Rapid City. I ran and ran and ran and ran. I ran until my lungs were burning and my legs were wet and screaming and my hands and ears were numb. I ran until I fell down into the snow, and then I stayed there on my hands and knees.

What now? *What now?*

I heard the snort of a horse and the muffled sound of hoofbeats against snow.

I didn't turn around, didn't get up off my hands and knees though my skin was burning from the cold. Actually, it was starting to feel warm. I was relieved he'd followed me, but I still didn't know what to do, so I stayed there and waited.

He hauled me to my feet by the belt loop of my pants, and he grabbed my arms and turned me to face him. For a second I thought he was going to kiss me, angry and hard. Something soft broke and leapt inside me.

He swore, yanked off his coat and wrapped it around me.

He put his gloves on me too, and his hat. When I tried to tell him not to, that he'd be cold, his eyes got mean, and he made this really garbled furious noise. I shut up.

"On the horse," he ground out, and hoisted me onto Chaucer. Then he came up after me.

We rode in silence to the house. I moved as little as possible, and I kept my eyes on the pommel. I was aware of blue night all around me, and I felt him shiver, and I shivered too, but I kept still. I didn't do much more than breathe until we were in the barn. I kept quiet as he helped me down.

He fucking tied me to a bolt on the wall.

He took my hands in his, and I thought he was going to say something to me, but the next thing I knew, he had rope wrapped around my wrists, and then my hands were above my head as he cinched me up good.

"Hey," I shouted, and then he gave me a glare, and I shut up.

He said nothing else, let me hang there while he saw to Chaucer. He fucking took his time too. When he came back to me, he still wouldn't look at me. He cut me down, but he didn't untie me, just grabbed the end of the rope and led me like a calf to the house.

The dogs were barking at the door, but Travis told them to go lie down, and they got silent in a way they rarely did. They watched me nervously, but I gave them a nod and tried to show I was okay.

I hoped I was.

HE LED ME to the basement.

I had mentioned I'd found the locked room in the basement and eventually gotten into it. In the time between the first tour and the night he found his presents, I had gotten several other and much more intimate tours of it.

I thought of it as the sex room. It wasn't very big, and it was clean and nice, but yeah. It was a sex room all right. That was where the fuck bench had come from, and it wasn't the only one. We'd had many a kinky night in the sex room. God, the toys.

One of my favorites was this impaler thing. He'd chain my wrists and ankles, and then he'd put me on the impaler. I held on to the sides so I didn't fall over, but my legs were spread and I was standing over this probe thing. It went up your ass, which is fine, but it is deliberately set a little too high. When you're on your tiptoes, it's okay, but if you relax your legs, it starts to get uncomfortable. Doesn't hurt you, just rubs you not quite the right way.

Travis would put me in this thing, then sit in front of me and ask me all sorts of dumbshit questions, usually about sheep or cows, or he'd tell me who had been in at the café that week when he'd gone for lunch, which he always did no matter what I left out for sandwiches. The game was I pretended I wasn't being impaled.

Eventually though he'd ask what was wrong, and then I had to tell him, graphically, about the thing in my ass. Then he would ask me what I'd rather have in there, and he'd show me all sorts of fucked-up implements. He wouldn't let me off the impaler until I said yes to at least three. And he picked up some scary shit, usually on purpose. He *always* picked up a baseball bat because he'd seen me freak out at one of the movies when one had gone up somebody's ass. He was never going to use it on me, we both knew it, but he enjoyed toying with me. And I liked being toyed with. It worked out.

Tonight was different. Tonight he was angry, and I was all fucked up. And I was coming down the stairs already tied up. Warning bells went off in my head, different ones than the ones that had been clanging since he'd shown up in the kitchen with the box. These were deeper, from a calmer place, but it wasn't calm now. *Maybe this isn't such a good idea.*

There are rules about playing. I break the one about don't be drunk a lot. I learned my lesson about being high, and I keep that one. But the big one is you don't do it pissed off at the other person. You don't play around with punishment stuff when you're actually angry. I guess I could see it in a relationship where you were okay and it was the way you dealt with a fuckup or misunderstanding. But we were fighting *about* the relationship. Or whatever this was. This was a bad, bad time to play pony or puppy or anything at all.

I was working up to say something when Travis turned around, slid a pocketknife through the binding of the rope and let the pieces fall to the floor. I was standing inside the door, and he turned away from me, walked across the room, sat in his chair and looked at me.

"Take off your clothes and sit on the bench."

He waited.

Turn. Go. Get out. Leave. Leave now. Go, get in your car, and go. Except I couldn't seem to move. I stared at Travis, sitting deep in his chair. He wasn't going to get up and come after me. If I left, he'd let me. Somehow I knew without being told. I could tell too if I said no, he wouldn't argue. It was still my safe word. He'd given me an order, but he was waiting to see if I accepted it.

We weren't playing. Yet. He was, in his way, asking if I wanted to.

I can't tell you why I didn't turn and go. I knew,

knew this was not what you were supposed to do, but I couldn't turn away from his face, and I couldn't leave. Some deeper part of me that didn't have words but knew how to move my body rose, carried me forward, took off my clothes, sat me on the bench and kept me there until he came over.

I wanted him to give me sex. I wanted him to open his fly and give me his cock. I wanted him to kiss me, lick me, fuck me, suck me. I wanted to pretend this hadn't happened. I wanted him to make it go away.

He gave me none of it. He reached for a paddle, held it up, and asked, "How many do you want?"

It wasn't a command. He might as well have been holding out cupcakes, asking how many I wanted. I could say I didn't care for any, thank you.

I swallowed hard, and then I said, "Four."

He gestured to the spanking bench. I shook a little as I walked over to it and knelt in place, but though I put my ankles and wrists against the restraints, he didn't close them. He waited until I was settled, then touched my lower back so I knew where he was.

"Ready?" he asked.

I nodded.

The first hit came down.

Paddles feel like blows. As if you should be shooting across the room, which is why, actually, you need the restraints. It was hard to not have them now. Not only did my whole body jerk and rattle as my ass bloomed into flame, but I felt like I was going to fall. After the second one, I summoned up enough breath to rasp, "Please tie me down."

He did, but the loops were so loose it wouldn't take much for me to get out, and they weren't fastened. I got the message. He wanted me to be able to go. But they kept me in place enough to receive the last two. My ass blazed. My body shook. But when he lowered the paddle, I felt empty.

"More, please," I whispered.

"How many?" His voice was both dispassionate and kind at once. It was strange.

"Four."

He delivered them with patience and skill, and I counted them out. My whole body pulsed when he finished. I didn't feel empty, but I didn't feel okay, either.

"More, please."

This time he hesitated.

"Please," I said again. "Just four more."

He didn't gentle them, but there was less urgency about these. The first four had been angry. The second four had bled his tension out of him. These last ones were for me. But between blows, he touched the small of my back. Asking me to please be done.

Either twelve was the right number or the touch pushed me over the edge. In any event, when he finished the last one and lowered the paddle, all I said was, "Thank you, Travis."

I had meant to say *sir*, but his name slipped out. He

stroked me lovingly. Then he set the paddle on a table and came to crouch in front of me. He looked tired. And sad.

"You never ask me about Riley," he said. "You only did that once."

Shrugging is hard when you're strapped to a spanking bench, but I did my best. "Not my business."

"Why isn't it your business?"

I sensed a trap, but I couldn't read him properly. I faltered. "He was with you before. Nothing I know about it changes anything between us."

Oh, and here he was, pissed again. "The same way your family treating you like dog shit doesn't change anything between us?"

I tried to jerk up, but of course now I was restrained. I frowned instead. "What the fuck is that supposed to mean?"

"What the fuck is you saying everything you do is shit supposed to mean? What is this bull about you being shit? Is *that* what you think of me? I'd share my life with someone I thought was shit?"

In the trap. Fucking in the center of the trap, and if I moved, it would close. I tugged at the straps, forgetting if I turned my hand, I could undo them. "I meant you shouldn't get pissed off about how I don't want to—" I was going to say *give you my garbage*, but I caught myself in time. I let out a frustrated sigh. "I am not as good as you or anybody else. Okay? I get that. I always have. Everybody's too nice to—" I broke off. This wasn't coming out like I meant.

His eyebrows went up. "Call you a piece of shit to your face?"

He had been joking, but when I lowered my head, embarrassed, he lifted my chin. I gave in and looked at him.

He was surprised. "You really mean it. You really do think you're garbage compared to other people." When I tried to turn my head away from him, he held my chin fast. "Roe. Monroe Harold Davis. You are not a piece of shit. You are not garbage. You are not less than anybody. In fact, I think you're probably better than most people I know. I know for a fact you're a better person than me."

I jerked away from him and pulled on the straps until they hurt. "Stop. *Stop. No!*"

The word echoed in the room. I'd never used it here. Never used it with him at all, not in a game. Not in sex. Not to tell him to quit.

I said it again. "No. *No.* No, no, no! Let me *out.* Let me go. Let me *go.*"

"You can undo the straps. They aren't tight." But he undid first one hand and then the other just the same. "I'm not playing, Roe. You can't toss a safe word at me when I'm saying you aren't crap. You don't get to tell me no when I'm telling you I care about you. You don't get to say stop when—"

"I love you."

It took me a few seconds to realize it'd been me

who had spoken. Out loud. To him. Now. Fucking now, here with me naked over a bench, after I screamed at him for telling me I wasn't garbage.

I panicked. I tried to push to my knees, but my arms wouldn't move. I looked at Travis, who stared at me.

I felt small. I didn't ache or hurt—except for my paddled ass—but I felt so small. Like a slight wind could knock me over. Like it could make me dissolve and fly away, up and out and over the fields.

I barely breathed. I just waited. Waited for him to speak. To move. To kiss me. To touch my face. To tell me he loved me too. Something. Anything.

He sat on his heels. "Riley ran."

Okay, to say something other than that.

He nodded in the general direction of the yard. "I went to Grand Island to pick up a part for a tractor. When I left, he was sulking in bed. When I came back, half the house was cleaned out, and there was a note on the kitchen table. *Since you hate my drama, I won't put you through an exit scene. Best of luck with the ranch.* That was it. No number. No address. He'd changed his email and his cell phone."

I frowned. That was pretty lousy. I know I'd done something similar to my family, but they'd kicked me out. It was different.

Travis continued. "I could've tracked him through the university, but he wasn't trying to hide from me. He was giving me *quiet* the way I always told him I needed. My space. Space without him in it. He left that way because he knew it would hurt. And it did."

He sighed. "I did want him around. I did love him. At least, I wanted to. I loved the idea of a partner out here in Nowhere. It hurt to have the one I'd chosen leave, especially in such a deliberately cruel manner."

"I would never leave like that," I whispered. He gave me a sharp look, but I shook my head. "It wasn't what I was doing."

"Oh no? What, you were running because you loved me?"

I couldn't bear to hear the hurt in him, so I drew a breath and said quietly, "Yes."

I was still kneeling, still naked, still burning from his blows. He crouched in front of me, staring, watching, but I couldn't see him now, not clearly. I couldn't see anything. I felt like I was glowing, as if the heat from his paddling had bloomed in my chest and opened it up, sending my heart out in front of me, hovering there before him.

Except there wasn't any terror now. There was just this. Me. Him. That word. Those other words. The waiting to see what he would do with them.

What he did was come forward, leaning until his knees met the floor, and then he walked to me on them, took my face in his hands and gave me a tender kiss against my lips.

"Don't run, ever again."

I forget how we got upstairs. He may have carried me. I remember we kissed the whole way. I remember falling onto the bed, his body covering me, and I remember arguing with him when he reached for a condom, saying I didn't want one. Saying I'd been tested before Rapid City and was okay. But he said no, he hadn't been tested in a while, but he would go on Monday.

I remember he made love to me. He whispered in my ear, and then because he'd asked so nice, I turned him over and made love to him right back. I remember curling up beside him, dick and ass humming and happy.

I remember him kissing my ear and saying, "I love you too, Roe."

The next morning I got out the box and showed him every piece. I explained what I had meant to do with them. I bit my tongue when I wanted to point out what was wrong with them. He wouldn't have listened anyway. He said they were all perfect. He was touched, I could tell. Pleased.

Loved.

He tried to wear them all at once, the idiot. I wouldn't let him, but he did insist on at least three. I have had to make him four belts since then, because he wears them out like crazy, since they're all he wears. The bracelet with his initials is usually on him too. But the circlet with the brand he gave back to me. He put it around my neck and told me it was to remind me I belonged at Nowhere and Nowhere belonged to me. Which I knew was his way of saying *he* belonged to me.

Which was what gave me the idea.

At Haley's next doctor appointment, I went down the street to the tattoo parlor with a piece of paper in my pocket. I came home with a slightly sore backside. After dinner I showed Travis.

He laughed. But it was a happy laugh. "You branded yourself with the Nowhere brand?"

"Yep," I told him. Then I touched the necklace. "For when I have to leave this off."

I got another kiss for that. Lots of them, actually.

Quite a few of them were on my new tattoo.

14

T HE PHONE CALL came in the middle of lambing.

Literally. I was out in the barn, my hand up a ewe trying to turn the lamb, when Travis came in and called my name.

"Bit busy, boss," I bit off, and got a better grip on the leg.

"Somebody take over for him," he said, and I looked up, wondering what the fuck, and I saw his face. I saw the phone in his hand.

I felt a cold wind blow across my neck.

I shooed off Paul and finished the lamb, but I did it in a daze. My ears rang as I went over to the sink to wash up. I kept my eye off Travis, but my mind didn't need my eyes to see him for it to tumble ahead and guess what this was about. I already knew who was on the phone. Well, I knew within three people. Probably two. That Travis had come into the barn during lambing narrowed it down to some grim options.

I took the phone from Travis. "'Lo."

"Hi, Roe. This is Bill."

"It's good to hear your voice." It was the truth. It was weird, but it was good. I waited for the rest.

"Sorry to interrupt. Lambing?"

"Yep. Had a breech, but it's okay now. Got her out. They can handle the rest without me." I cleared my throat and fought against the pit forming in my stomach as I gave him his opening. "What can I do for you?"

A pause. The longest, most hollow pause in the world, so loud it muffled the bleating of the ewes and lambs.

"Dad passed away."

You can't be ready for someone to tell you one of your parents is gone. I found out it doesn't even matter if you parted on bad terms and had decided it was better not to restart relations. It didn't matter, not at that moment. Death changes everything.

When I was able, I asked, "When?"

"Couple of hours ago." There was another pause. It was heavy, and when Bill spoke, I could tell each word was a lead weight on him. "I wasn't watching close enough. He got the keys and tried to drive into town."

I shut my eyes and didn't say anything.

"The good thing," Bill went on, his voice shaky, "is he didn't hurt anybody else. You remember the concrete median at the T-intersection by Coppit Corner? He hit it at about sixty-five. They said he died instantly, or real close."

He paused, like it was my turn, but I didn't know

what to say. What did you say when your brother, whose voice you hadn't heard in five years, called and said your dad had died?

My dad. My dad was dead. I would never see him again. Ever.

I stared straight ahead of me, but I didn't see a thing. The last words he'd said to me had been "Get the north forty done." After that all I got was looks of disappointment and revulsion. They would be all I ever got.

There was no more Dad. The thought kept rolling over and over in my head, stuck. *No more Dad. No more Dad. No more Dad.*

"I was hoping you would come home for the funeral," Bill said.

I cleared my throat and shuffled my feet. "Yeah." Then it hit me what "coming home" would involve. "You sure?"

"That I want you home for our father's funeral? Yes, Roe. I'm damn sure."

I could tell already this was going to be grim from the tone of his voice. I saw Travis move out of the corner of my eye, and I turned, finally, and met his gaze.

Sometimes it hits me how patient Travis is. He knew about my dad, I realized, because he wouldn't have given Bill to me for anything less. And he wasn't leaving my side until he figured out how I was. He didn't know what to say, either. But he was there. Waiting.

"Whatever you need," Travis said, "we do. You need to go home, we go. Whenever and for however long." I glanced at the lambs and opened my mouth to object, but he overrode me. "Tory can handle it. If you want to go, find out the details, and we'll get ready to head out."

We.

It hit me he kept saying *we. We* will go. Not me. He wasn't offering, either. He was going, if I was.

I reached out, fingers shaking. He met my hand halfway, and he gripped it tight. I felt his strength come into me, and I think I took my first real breath in ten minutes.

"Roe?" Bill said into my ear.

I looked right into Travis's eyes. "I'm coming."

We were coming.

HALEY CAME WITH us too.

She was seven months pregnant and then some, gone from cute little baby belly to as big as a fucking house. Both Travis and I told her no, she should stay home, as did her mother and her father, the latter with an emphasis shaking the very earth.

She came anyway.

"I have my records," she said as we got in the truck to go and I tried, one last time, to get her to stay home. "I have my entire medical file. I know the number of every hospital between here and Algona. I have a cell phone. I also have a month and a half to go. You're talking about a few days."

All I could think of were the million things that could go wrong. "Haley, this is going to be some sonofabitch thing where we're at the funeral and my family starts fighting and you go into labor in the middle of it."

"You told me your family doesn't fight, they just give long, cold stares."

"Well, I figure you're going to pick a fight!"

She shrugged. "Maybe. Maybe not. And if I do go into labor, I go into labor. They have babies in Iowa too, I'm almost sure of it."

There was no reasoning with her. There was certainly no arguing with her. So she came along.

Of course, because she came along, we stopped a hell of a lot more for bathroom breaks. We had to head into South Dakota to get on I-90, and we took it into southern Minnesota to Highway 71 and then the smaller roads wound us in to Algona. The trip took nine hours without stopping on a good day, but it was a solid twelve for us because of all the rest breaks. By the time we hit the Super 8, it was ten o'clock at night.

It was hard to be home. It had gotten harder with every mile that brought us closer. As soon as we hit the Iowa border, I really started to itch. In Algona itself, I felt every eye on me. I thought of how they would know about how I was coming from Nebraska, and we were in Travis's truck, so the plates said Nebraska, and they'd know it was me. They'd be talking about me already.

I shouldn't have come back. I should've stayed at the ranch.

The desk clerk at the Super 8 saw me come through the door, and she smiled a sad smile and came at me with her arms open.

"Roe Davis. My word, how many years has it been? So sorry to hear about your dad, hon. He was a good man." She cottoned on that I was a stiff board in her arms, and she withdrew and gave me a laugh. "You don't remember me, do you? It's Missy Letts. We were in school together. I was one grade behind you. You sat beside me in freshman English."

I blinked, trying to remember. I had been high through most of freshman English both times I took it. "Oh," I said, trying to pretend. "Sure."

Her face was round and shiny, but when she saw Haley, it got rounder and shinier as she beamed. "Ooh, and is this your wife? Oh my word, and you're going to be a daddy."

I wanted to run so bad. Travis must have figured it out, because his hand came down on my shoulder. Haley, arms folded over her belly, gave the clerk her *I'm nice, but don't fuck with me* smile.

"No. My boyfriend knocked me up and ran. I'm Haley, Roe's friend." She nodded at Travis. "This is Travis Loving. Roe's partner."

Travis's hand tightened, keeping me in place. I swallowed hard and waited.

Missy Letts's eyes had gone wide. Her mouth had

fallen open, and for a second we all stared at one another, me terrified, Missy shell-shocked, Travis probably blank as a slate, and Haley making it clear anybody fucking with me would be answering to her.

Carefully composing herself, Missy smiled again. "Well, that will teach me to go assuming things, won't it?" She let out a breezy, slightly nervous sigh and patted me on the arm. "It's good to see you, Roe." She winked at Travis. "And your partner is a handsome one. Good catch."

Then she bustled around to the other side of the desk, and as if she met up with gay dropouts who'd sat beside her in freshman English every day, she booked us our rooms, asking us if we wanted adjoining, upgrading Haley's for no charge with a wink and a smile to a suite with a whirlpool tub in it. "For your back, hon. I remember that stage. Don't make it too hot, but soak as much as you want. And make these big, strong boys carry all your luggage."

I was ready to get upstairs, but Haley kept us in the lobby, asking about Missy's kids, about doctors in town "just in case." To my annoyance, she kept dragging the conversation to me and Travis.

"It's so wet here," she said, amazed. "It rained all the way down from Minnesota, and from the look of it, that's all it's done all week. We don't get much of it in northwest Nebraska." She nodded at Travis. "You could use some of this rain on the ranch, I bet."

It was such a blatant *hey, Roe's man has a ranch* brag I

wanted to kick her, pregnant or not. But Missy ate it up, because this was good dish. She turned to Travis with new appraisal.

"Oh-ho. Handsome *and* has a ranch? How big is your spread?"

"Seven hundred head of American Beltie and six-fifty head of Merino on three thousand acres," he replied. "Can't make up my mind if I want to stick to one or the other, so I keep expanding both."

To Iowans, that kind of acreage sounded like a king must run it, and Missy gave me a look saying, *Don't let this one go, boy.*

I opened my mouth to tell her this was a hobby ranch, but Haley had taken over. "Roe started out as a hand there. My dad is the manager, and he says nobody knows sheep the way Roe does."

Started out? I still *was* a hand.

Missy smiled and nodded. "Oh, yes. The Davises have always been good farmers. In the blood, see."

It was another ten minutes before we got to get our things and go upstairs. We had to take a few trips to get the cooler and everything, and when I passed through the lobby to head to the elevator, I saw Missy on the phone in the office, speaking intently and waving her hands at the wall in excitement as she spoke.

I didn't know who she was calling, but I knew exactly what she was saying.

"Don't worry about it." Haley lingered in the doorway between our rooms. "You're here for your family.

For your dad."

"My family ain't going to care for those rumors flying around," I told her. "Dad wouldn't either."

"Tough," she said, kissed me on the cheek, and then closed the door.

I heard the tub water start to run shortly after. I got undressed, showered and lay down on the bed beside Travis, who was surfing the Internet on his laptop. When I leaned into him, he shifted his arm to pull me in tighter. "You doing okay?"

I shrugged. "I don't know. I feel like I'm in a dream. Any second you're going to wake me up and tell me it's time to go start lambing. Tell me this isn't real."

He sighed and pressed his lips to my hair. "It's real."

My fingers skimmed up his shirt and toyed idly with the buttons. "I don't know what I'm supposed to do tomorrow when we go over. Don't know what to say."

His hand rubbed my back gently. "You'll work it out. From what you tell me, they won't make so much of a fuss with Haley and me there. And I won't leave your side unless you ask. And even then you might have to ask twice."

I swallowed hard and let my finger slip between the gap of his shirt panels, touching the hair on his chest. "I love you." It still stuck in my throat a little, but it was getting easier to say.

He kissed the top of my hair again. "Love you more."

15

I N THE MORNING we got up, got dressed, hit the continental breakfast and tried to ignore the eager looks and whispers from the day desk staff. I didn't know anyone, but they clearly had all the dish from Missy. They weren't glaring at me, though. They acted like I was some kind of celebrity.

That wasn't the case when we got out to the farm.

Heading down our gravel road was the hardest part of the trip. I was sitting in the backseat, which I had done the whole trip because Haley needed the space unless she was trying to nap, but holy shit, it was good I was in the back now. I think if I'd been in the front, I would have tried to jump out the door.

I turned away at Coppit Corner, but not in time. I saw the shattered concrete of the median, saw the wreath somebody had hung there, and I shut my eyes, shaking, not knowing how I was ever going to get through this.

Haley grabbed my hand.

I got a lot of hand-holding and mumbled comforting words of nonsense. It's all kind of silly, but there's nothing else to say or do, really. People hold your hand while you grieve. Not because they're trying to pretend things are okay. They mean things will go on. That you will too. Which, at the moment, isn't what you want. You want things to stop. You want to take ten minutes or maybe ten days or even ten years and figure this out, but no, everything keeps going. And going. And going.

That day, I had to keep going, and Haley and Travis helped me. I went up the sidewalk to the house I had lived in from the time I was born until they'd kicked me out of it. I walked with my lover's hand on the small of my back and my pregnant Amazon warrior friend flanking me.

I walked up to my mom, who was standing in the doorway looking at me. Smiling. Crying.

My heart soared.

Then I realized she was looking at Haley too, and my heart crashed. She was doing what Missy Letts had done. She thought I wasn't just coming home but coming home straight and with a pregnant wife. I thought of the look of devastation that was about to cross her face, my heart dove into my feet, and the next thing I knew, I was turning around and heading down the sidewalk.

Travis stopped me, but I shook my head. "I can't. I can't watch her hate me again." I shut my eyes and pressed my hand over my chest because it hurt so bad.

"Haley's talking to her." Travis had both hands on me now, one on my arm, one on my back. "Just keep breathing. We're both right here. Take it easy." He kept on rubbing, and I kept on breathing as best I could until he squeezed my arm. "Okay. Haley's motioning to us. Come on, Roe. You can do it."

I was wearing my felt cowboy hat, and he tipped it forward a little as was his way, a playful nudge. He'd done it a thousand times in front of everybody, but all I could think was my mom was watching. Was she seeing my lover, my partner taking care of me, or was she seeing me as an abomination? I didn't want to find out. But I had to.

I didn't look at her until I got to the porch, until I was staring at her shoes—dirty, worn-out orthopedic white shoes with navy socks.

Holding my breath, I glanced up.

I wish I could tell you it was some magical moment. I wish I could tell you Haley had worked it out, that Mom was so glad to see me she didn't care who I loved. I wish I could tell you I was welcomed like the prodigal son. But I can't tell you that and be honest.

Oh, she didn't yell. In fact, she was very polite. She smiled. Cried a little more and hugged me.

But Missy at the Super 8 had hugged me harder.

Bill was inside, as was his wife. He hugged me, stiff and awkward, then looked at Haley with his eyebrows up. Funny how the rumor was probably all over town, but everybody would have worked hard not to mention it to my family. So Haley told the story again. She was getting good at it. I wished she would leave off the *Roe's partner* bit, because I never turned away in time.

Though I will say I enjoyed watching Bill and Travis get puffed up around each other. Talk about a pissing contest. Bill was clearly trying to look down at this sleazy bastard having dirty gay sex with his little brother, and Travis, who had ten years, five inches and fifteen hundred acres on Bill, didn't so much as flinch, only stared down at his lover's homophobic brother.

We sat around the table in the kitchen. Bill's wife served everybody coffee and some of the food people had brought by, and we played nice. Bill and Travis talked cattle, about the difference between Iowa and Nebraska land management, and then they dragged me into some talk about sheep.

For a while it was almost as if we were normal. Bill wanted to know about the Merino wool market and how that worked out, and Travis talked about the profit margin, and I talked about the dos and don'ts of organic wool regulation. I was back home. At the kitchen table, with my family.

Mom wiped at her eyes and avoided my gaze. She acted like Travis wasn't even there. But she kept looking at Haley, especially at her belly. I wondered if Bill had 'fessed up about not being able to have his own kids yet. I wondered if she was looking at Haley's belly and thinking about all she wasn't going to have. I wondered if she was blaming me for taking it away from her by being gay.

We finished lunch, and after that a few people stopped by, mostly from the church with more food. You could kill yourself on the food in the house already, but it kept coming, because that was the way it was. Half of it would have to be thrown out. Sarah packed up as much as she could to send with us when we left for the hotel.

Haley made me sit in the front seat, and she rubbed my shoulders all the way into town.

"You did good, Roe," she said. "You did real good."

Back at the Super 8, Haley took a nap, and even though I told Travis I wasn't tired, I did too. And then it was five, and we had to head over to the funeral parlor for the visitation.

The director gave us all a few moments alone with Dad's body, and without anybody arranging it out loud, Mom and Bill and Sarah went in first, and then Travis and Haley and I went in after on our own.

It wouldn't be an open casket because of the accident, but it was open now. It was pretty grim, but I had to do it. In my mind Dad wasn't all the way dead yet. I kept thinking he would come through the door and correct me on something or tell Travis to get the fuck away from his son. Something. Anything. I couldn't make my brain believe. I needed to see it for myself.

It was bad. He had a big, crazy, stitched-up scar down the center of his face, and part of it was out-and-out covered up. His skin was white. Paper white. His lips looked wrong too. Everything was wrong about him. I mean, everything. It wasn't him. This wasn't the man whose strides I tried to match when we went out to do chores. This wasn't the man who'd hefted me up on his shoulders so I could see the Fourth of July parade. This wasn't the man who'd tanned my backside for hiding my report card in the bottom of the wastebasket. This wasn't a man at all. It was just a body.

It's funny how there's things you have to do. You have to go up and touch his hand. You have to bend down and kiss his forehead, even if you're scared to death the drape is going to slide and you're going to see something that will make you throw up.

You have to take your lover's hand and hold it tight while you say, "I love you, Dad." You have to feel like when you turn away, a part of you has died too, the part of you sure, absolutely sure this could not be right, that your dad had not kicked you out without a word and not spoken to you for years and then died without saying you were okay as who you were.

Kayla was there when we came out from viewing Dad, and Pastor Tim was with her.

We stayed away from each other during the wake. Haley and Travis flanked me, though everybody kept making Haley sit down. I think I shook three hundred people's hands. I said "Thank you for coming" over and over.

Every now and again somebody looked at Travis and then back at me expectantly, wanting the story, but

I was so numb I never gave it. Haley didn't say anything either, though sometimes Travis did. He doesn't care for talking about feelings, but he gossips like an old biddy, and he fit right in once he got warmed up. He yammered on about ranching, about teaching math at college, and when Harold Yomer came through, he even got on his Libertarian spiel.

Oh, some people skipped right over us, pretending we weren't there. I didn't mind at all. Less talking for me.

When we finally got through the whole line and it was time to go, Kayla came over, dragging Pastor Tim and looking purposeful, but Haley herded us toward the door, and when Kayla tried to stop us, Haley said she wasn't feeling well and touched her belly. The grandmother brigade started to cluck and fuss, and we were out the door in minutes.

Once we were at the hotel, I lay awake on the bed staring at the ceiling in the dark.

Travis lay on his side beside me, and he touched my shoulder. "Still doing okay?"

I kept my eyes on the ceiling. "It's weird, how Kayla and Haley are so much the same and so different at the same time. I mean, they even look alike."

"Haley smiles more."

I grabbed his hand in the dark. "I'm glad you both came."

"Wouldn't be anywhere else."

"I just hope she doesn't have a baby during the funeral."

"From your mouth to God's ears." He kissed my cheek, then turned my face so he could get to my lips. "It's going to be okay, Roe."

I nodded, and I kissed him again.

Then it was morning, and the funeral.

It was the same as the visitation, except everything felt heavier. I shook a lot of hands and got hugs from old ladies. I sat in a pew and listened to a lot of prayers and Bible verses and people blowing their noses.

I stood at the front left corner of my father's casket, and I carried it down the aisle of the church, down the stairs to the hearse, and then I rode to the cemetery.

At two thirty in the afternoon on April 21, I helped work the cinch and put my father's body in the ground.

We went to the farm after. There were fewer people there than at the funeral, but it was pretty full, and while Haley chatted up my aunt Carol, and Travis stood sentry against the kitchen wall, I slipped up the stairs to my old room.

Everything was still there.

It was a relief, but it was creepy too, because it was exactly as it had been when I left. Someone came in regularly and vacuumed and dusted, but everything I had left behind was here. The ribbon from a demo derby I'd entered and won was on the bulletin board. My magazines—the clean ones—were in the bookcase in my headboard. My CDs were lined up neat along the top of my desk, propped up by the Pink Floyd mirror I had won at the state fair when I was ten. The clothes I hadn't taken with me were hanging in the closet. It was all here, like I had been gone five minutes, not five years.

I didn't hear anyone come up the stairs, only Pastor Tim's voice from the doorway. "They still love you, Roe."

I turned around, caught, but Pastor just gave me his patient smile and held out his hands.

"They love you, Roe. They always have. All you have to do is turn away from the darkness and come back into their loving arms, into the light of Christ."

Kayla appeared beside him. She wasn't smiling. "Don't put your family through any more, Roe. Don't hurt them any more than they already are."

I stood there frozen, but I wasn't scared. I was tired. So tired. I didn't want this anymore. I couldn't be scared or upset because I didn't have anything left in me. I figured I would suck it up until they were done, and then I'd kiss my mom and shake my brother's hand and go home.

I had forgotten about Haley.

One minute Kayla was several paragraphs into a lecture about the state of my soul and how unfair I was to my mom and my brother, and the next minute I saw Haley behind her, looking at the back of Kayla's head like she was ready to rip it off. I opened my mouth and started forward in alarm.

Kayla held up a hand. "I'm not finished."

"Oh yes you are, bitch," Haley said, and pushed Kayla into the room.

16

"Ladies!" Pastor Tim cried out, but Haley turned on him, and he shut up fast.

Haley pointed at the two of them. "I'm assuming you're Kayla the cousin and Tim the pastor. That right?" She waited for murmurs of acknowledgment, and once she had them, she nodded and cut them off again. "Got it. Just wanted to be sure. I came a long way to see the two of you. Wanted to make sure I was shouting at the right people."

"Listen." Kayla was back on her feet and pissed as hell, but Haley rounded on her, pregnant belly and everything.

"No, *you* listen. You too, Pastor. You listen, and you listen fucking good. You get your ears turned all the way on, because today *I* have the gospel for you, and you had better fucking take notes."

"Your language," Pastor Tim sputtered.

"Yeah, that's a good place to start. Language. I don't care for yours. I don't like the way you talk down to

Roe, how you fill him full of bullshit and hate and guilt until he can't move. You tell Roe he's the abomination, you tell him he's hurting his family, you tell him he's a sinner going to hell because of who he loves."

She huffed angrily through her nose. "Doesn't that even grab at you for a second? Are you so dead inside he can come home with *the man he loves* and you can only give him a bunch of badly translated words? All day you've been looking at Roe like Satan himself has appeared and you're ready to stake him and shove him back to hell. Which is nothing but a heap of shit. Roe is a good man. He is one of the best men I've ever met. He's kind. He's courteous. He's loyal, and he's strong. And I love him. Everybody at Nowhere loves him."

Haley indicated my confirmation picture on the wall. "Love. That's what I was taught being Christian meant. I was taught Jesus wanted us to love everyone. He was the original hippie, turning everything on its ear so we could open up and love each other not just now but forever. The one who hung out with whores and lepers and tax collectors. The guy with story after story about social pariahs as heroes and heroines. The one who talked about how 'loving the least of those is loving me.' The one who told the story of the fucking prodigal son. *Love*." She shook her head. "You don't love him. What you're doing to Roe isn't love."

"Sometimes love is hard." Pastor Tim was red-faced and angry. "God was angry with his people when they turned away, and like him, we—"

"The cranky, pouty God is in the Old Testament, Timmy, and if you're going to get literal on me, if you're going to say we can't piecemeal the Bible, then I want to know how you rationalize your hate with Jesus saying *love one another* trumps everything. And I want to know how much bacon you shovel down your throat, you hypocrite."

"Levitical law is based—"

"*You can't pick and choose!*" She was almost on top of him now, literally backing him into the corner. "You can't say you need to burn witches and shun gay men then eat all the pork and wear all the mixed fibers you want. You don't get to say loving him means turning his family against him so soundly he never got to make peace with his dad. You don't get to tell me your vision of the Bible is divinely inspired, letting you fill so many people with so much fucking hate in his name."

"*Get away from him.*" Kayla raised her fist.

From the second Haley started swearing, I was in a kind of shock. It was a dream, and I was sure I was going to wake up and have to do the funeral again, this time without Haley bursting in as pregnant Wonder Woman. While she shouted and Tim sputtered, I just stood there, gobsmacked, not knowing what I was supposed to do.

But I listened. I listened to her defense of me, to her lecture about Tim and God and love. I wasn't sure all of it was right, what she was doing. It felt good to be defended, but this wasn't the way. Hate against hate and shouting over shouting wasn't going to help. There had to be a middle way.

I listened, and I watched. Watched Tim, watched Kayla, watched Haley. I saw the way Kayla looked at Haley. The way she looked at Tim, the possession in her gaze, and I thought, whoa.

Then I saw her fists clench and her body go taut right before she threw herself at Haley, and because I'd been watching, I was moving before she was.

I stepped between her and Haley. I raised my arm and took the blow she'd meant for my friend. It came down hard on my left shoulder and cut into my neck. It would have come across Haley's cheek, would have knocked her into the hall toward the top of the stairs. It hit me how much that could have hurt Haley and the baby, and now it was me looking down at Kayla with cold hate. "Get out."

Her face twisted into rage, and she reared back.

I said it again. Louder. "Get the fuck out of my room. Get out of my house. And don't you *ever* try to lay a hand on my friend."

I felt a hand on my shoulder. I knew by the weight and the way his fingers curled into my collarbone that it was Travis.

Pastor Tim took Kayla's arm and spoke soothingly to her. "It's time to go. There will be another day, another time."

"No there won't," Haley said, still sparking for her fight, but Travis murmured, "That's enough," and Kayla and Tim left the room and headed down the stairs without further incident.

Once we heard the front door open and close, Travis herded us down too.

My mom was at the bottom of the stairs.

She didn't say anything, but as I gave her a quick, uneasy hug, I saw her looking at Haley wide-eyed. My sister-in-law watched Haley too, but she had a lightness that surprised me. She gave me a full smile, kissed my cheek and urged me, with heartfelt sincerity, to keep in touch.

I shook my brother's hand without really meeting his eye.

We drove to the hotel in silence. Part of the way, anyway.

"That," Travis said eventually, "was really stupid, Haley."

"I don't care." Haley stared out the window. "They deserved it and more."

"Yes, but if Roe hadn't stepped forward when he did, you could have been hurt. You and the baby both."

She shrugged, but she also rested her head on my arm hanging over the seat. I kissed the top of her head and shut my eyes, breathing in the smell of her hair.

AT THE HOTEL, Haley went to her room for a bath, and in ours, Travis pulled out a bottle of whiskey. He poured liberal amounts in two plastic hotel glasses and passed one to me.

"When your father is dead, you drink whiskey," he told me.

"That a law?" I asked.

"It's what I did." He downed his glass.

I did too. Three shots later I said, "I forgot your dad was dead too. I guess we don't talk about your family much. Sorry." I rubbed my foot against his leg.

He reached over and stroked my thigh, and then he poured me more whiskey.

When the bottle was half gone, we fell into bed. I told him, drunkenly, that I loved him. He sucked on my ear and told me he loved me more. We kissed for a while, and then we drank some more, and then he blew me. After, we drank some more.

When the bottle was three-quarters gone, I started to cry.

It came up out of nowhere, and to be honest I scared myself. One minute I was shoving my toe into Travis's armpit, slurring and laughing as I tried to tell him the story of how I had crashed my bike at the end of my drive and tore my leg up so bad it had flaps of skin pulled back, but all I could think about was how mad Dad would be that I bent the frame, and I bled the whole way to the garage and passed out trying to fix it with a vise.

Suddenly I was doubled over and sobbing.

I bawled. I had never cried like that before in my life, and I haven't cried like that since. Once in junior high we read a story about a woman keening, and the teacher had explained the word to us saying it was a terrible grief, the kind that tore at your soul. I always thought of it when I thought of my mom crying about not being able to have more babies. There in the Super 8, sloppy drunk on cheap whiskey, stinking from sex, wrapped in the arms of my lover, I keened too.

I keened for my dad. For all he had been, for all he would now never be. For the way I had never come back and tried to make things right with him. For his being sick too young, for him being so frustrated by his disease he risked his life and anybody else's who might have met him on the road.

I keened for the years we had lost. For the farming I never got to do for him. For never being able to tell him about the work I'd done at Nowhere. For never being able to show him what a good man I'd become after all.

I keened, more than anything, for me. For letting so many years of my life go by in silence, for not being able to understand for so long what Haley and Travis and Tory had seen so quickly. I was never the devil, and I didn't deserve to be treated like one. Hate can never be love, not for any excuse.

I keened for going through so much of my life never having friends because I didn't think I was good enough to have any. I keened for being so afraid of love that if it looked like I might find it, I ran.

I keened for all of it, keened until I choked on the tears and then, inevitably, I threw up.

Travis held my head over the toilet by my hair until

I could come up with nothing more than dry heaves. He showered me and wrapped me up in his arms in the dark. When it was all still, when he pressed sweet kisses into my temple, I cried again. No more keening, just quiet, steady tears as I thanked the grace of the God who had seen fit, despite my efforts and those of my family, to put me safely in this man's arms.

In the morning I woke to silence.

I could hear the fan on the air conditioner on the other side of the room and the occasional footsteps in the hall outside, but the air was full of stillness. It wasn't quite sad. Shaded a little, maybe. But not melancholy.

Inside me was quiet too. I didn't feel empty and hollow the way I had, but I didn't feel full either. I'd buried my dad and cried until I got sick, and yet I was still here. My family had thrown me out and hurt me, and I'd gone to prison and then gone all across the Midwest—but I was still here. I had cut people out and then brought them in, and I was still here.

My father was dead. But I was alive.

Something stirred in me, waking. It felt like that angel who had whispered to me before, who had told me to stay. The morning after we buried my dad, the angel woke, all the way for real, and I was stunned to find out the angel inside me wasn't an angel at all.

It was me.

I turned in Travis's arms, buzzing with a quiet energy now. I wrapped my arms around him as best I could, and I kissed his chest. I actually kind of felt good.

Maybe it wasn't polite to feel so good right then, with my dad fresh in the ground, but I did feel good. So good I wanted to laugh. I wanted to run out across the highway into the park and dance around naked. I was here. I was okay. I was alive.

I didn't run across the highway. I didn't get out of bed. I opened my mouth over the hairy center of my lover's chest, and I kissed him.

In less than five minutes he was fully awake and dragging me up to his mouth, kissing me back. We were both hard, both ready, but we lingered over the kissing like it was the only thing in the world. We might have kissed for fifteen minutes. Maybe half an hour. All the while I bubbled and built up inside, and eventually I dragged him on top of me and lifted my legs in invitation. He reached over onto the bedside table.

He came back only with lube.

We'd gotten the all-clear results from the tests the week before, but there hadn't been time for anything but quick jerk offs before bed with all the lambing, and without arranging it out loud, I knew we were both waiting for the right moment.

This felt like the right moment now. It felt right when he slicked us both up and then pushed inside me—just him, nothing else, nothing but skin on skin. It felt good, and it felt right, and it must have felt that way for him too because it wasn't long before he was coming hard and fast inside me.

I felt him. I felt his spunk, felt it coating my insides.

I imagined parts of him would be there forever, merging into my skin. I felt some of the semen leaking out, and when he withdrew, I tried to reach down quick and hold it in place, to keep it in.

But his hand got there first, and he smiled as he pressed his fingers flush against my rim. "I told you," he said, voice rough but not unkind. "I know what you want, and I give it to you."

He kept his hand there as he jerked me off, his fingers firmly in place, and I came like a geyser. His mouth came down on mine, and I kissed him, loved him, welcomed him. My lover. My partner.

My Travis.

WE GOT A late start the next day, and this time Haley did most of the driving. At one point Travis was snoring in the backseat, and I leaned over on Haley's shoulder. My hand rested on her belly as I waited to feel the baby kick.

"I didn't have the baby at the funeral," she pointed out.

"Hush. We still have nine hours yet until we're home."

"It's not going to happen today."

She was right. The baby didn't come that day. She came at two fifteen in the afternoon on May twenty-fifth.

17

I WAS SHEARING, had just got the wether wrestled where I wanted him, when Travis appeared in the door.

"Haley's heading to the hospital."

Both Tory and I stood up at the same time, and the wether, sensing his moment, bleated and scurried away. I dropped the shears, vaulted over the rail and headed for the door, where Ez and Zeke met me and barked excitedly all the way to the house.

"It's going to be hours," Travis told me, but I ignored him and bolted for the shower.

We got to the hospital just before noon. Haley was dilated five centimeters.

Her mom was her birthing coach, but Haley had asked me to be there too, and so there I was. I thought I might catch some hell or be told to scrub down, but nope, they let us all in. Travis tried to stay out because it was so crowded, but Haley got mad.

"No, I want you both here," she said, and so we

stayed.

We held her hands while she pushed, me on one side and Travis on the other. Travis looked fucking scared, and he didn't say much, so I did the talking this time, telling Haley she could do it, telling her she was beautiful, telling her she was strong and amazing, and it was almost over. I told her it was going to be okay. She was going to have a beautiful baby girl who was going to kick tail all over the state of Nebraska like her mom.

Then, all of a sudden, there was a head, and then, pop, it was a baby.

At first, to be honest, she was gross and kind of scary. But then Haley's mom cut the cord, and they cleaned her up, and then they wrapped the baby up and brought her to Haley, and my God, but she was the most beautiful thing in the world.

Haley cried. She kissed her baby, and she cried, and then she kissed me and kissed Travis, and she cried some more.

Then she turned to the two of us and said, "I want you to have her."

At first I thought it must be the drugs. I glanced at Travis, worried, but he was looking at her with a strange expression, something between wonder and terror.

Haley sat up straighter and said in an even stronger voice, "I want the two of you to have her. I want you to adopt her, and I want you to be her parents."

I sat down on the chair behind me and held on to the rail of her bed.

There had never been any decision about what she was going to do with the baby. I knew she wasn't happy with any of the adoption agencies, and her mom had thrown her a shower, so I'd assumed, like everybody else, Haley was keeping her. Never in a thousand years did I think she'd ask Travis and me.

But I knew the look in her eye, and I knew the tone in her voice. She'd been plotting this. When I glanced over Travis's shoulder and saw Haley's mom, I knew we were some of the last people to know about Haley's little plan.

"If you don't want her, I'm going to keep her," she said matter-of-factly, but I could tell she was nervous. "I want to be able to see her grow up. I'd rather have her settled in a home with two parents, would rather give her up so I can go to school and become a teacher and meet somebody who's not a loser and have a kid when I'm married and established, but I have to know she's with really good people, and you two are the best I know. But if you don't want a baby, if this is too much, you can just be her godfathers." She shifted the baby in her arms and looked down. "I didn't want to ask until you saw her. I thought maybe if she was in front of you it would be different. But obviously, you'll want to think about it. To talk. That's what I want, though. I want to give my baby to you. To both of you." She swallowed hard and gave a watery smile. "I'd rather you were married, but you know. One step at a time."

We had never discussed this. Ever. I never figured

I'd be a father, not after I knew I couldn't be with a woman. I was having a hard time even landing on the idea.

A father? Me?

A father with Travis?

With Haley's baby.

A soft coo drew my attention, and I stared at the bundle in Haley's arms. Her face was wrinkled like an old woman. But those eyes. They were dark, dark blue, and I know she couldn't really see, but she was staring at me. Her nose was small and squished, her head was freakishly pointed, and her skin was blotchy, but those eyes cut into my soul.

Not even fifteen minutes old, alive and here, Haley's baby nobody had planned for and yet was here all the same. Haley's little girl who, just like me, didn't have a daddy.

I reached out tentatively. I put my finger to her fist, nudging it against her fingers.

They opened, then closed fast around me, those eyes still fixed on mine.

I turned to Travis.

He was looking at the baby, still terrified, but his terror was bleeding away, leaving behind mostly wonder and quiet surprise. And a bit of longing.

I knew we were going to say yes.

We would worry if we had done the right thing. We would flail around trying to get ready and doubt ourselves a thousand times. We would call Haley's mom a lot, probably in the middle of the night. We'd have piles to learn.

But as Travis reached out and worked his finger inside the little girl's other hand, I knew we were going to keep her.

WE NAMED HER Grace May Davis-Loving.

For the first three months, Haley lived with us. We threw together a quick nursery in the upstairs bedroom, and it was Haley's room too. She nursed the baby most of the time, but once she went to school in the fall, she switched over to formula, because she had a tough time keeping up with the milk. Once she got busy with classes, we decided it was best for everybody if we out-and-out switched over. Haley moved to her parents' house, which was hard for everybody. She came over every day, but it wasn't the same.

That summer I also finished my GED online. I passed on the first try, and it really wasn't so bad. They said my essays were some of the best they'd seen.

We had to hire more hands because Travis expand-ed the operation in the fall, and though I still was the go-to man for sheep, I had my hands full with Grace. Travis and I took turns, but it isn't as if he sits in the office all day and plays solitaire. So we had to get more hands. I oversaw the shearing with Grace strapped in a sling in front of me, but mostly I was out of ranching for a while.

There were days it was really hard, having a baby. At

least once a week I wondered what the hell I had gotten myself into. But I loved her. I loved her heart and soul, and I would never give her up.

Sometimes I stood at the side of her crib and watched her sleep, still amazed she was even there. I stood there and thought of what I'd been doing a year ago, and I couldn't believe it.

She was real. It was real. All this, all my life, had become real.

Then came Thanksgiving.

Haley had been acting odd for a while. I thought it was because she was nervous about switching over to UNL in January, about leaving Grace behind, but no, it was more than that. Haley had been up to her tricks again. Because when I heard the front door open as Grace screamed in her bouncy seat and the dogs barked as I wrangled the turkey onto the plate, I shouted for Travis to get in here and help me, and I heard Haley call back, "It's not Travis."

"Well, you get in here then," I said.

She came around the corner, and I looked at her, impatient. Then I saw her face, and I stilled.

"It's not just me." She stepped aside.

There was my brother. And my sister-in-law.

And my mom.

She was bent more than she'd been when I'd seen her in April, and she looked like she'd aged seven years, not seven months. But then Grace screamed again.

My mom's eyes lit up, and years fell away. She scurried forward like an arthritic spider, dodging the dogs, and she bent down, undid the strap to the bouncy seat, and she took my daughter in her arms.

"Haley sends us photos." Bill slid up beside me. He tucked his hands into his jeans pockets. "Mom gets a letter about once a week, full of pictures of her granddaughter." He glanced nervously at me. "I hope it's okay that we came. Haley said it was fine, but I can tell from your face you weren't expecting us."

No, I fucking wasn't. Not in a million years.

I watched my mom nuzzle Grace's nose, and I heard my daughter laugh and reach for her grandmother's face. I thought of the collection of pink hats and knew she had a bag full of them in the car.

"It's not a problem at all. God knows we have more than enough food." I cleared my throat and turned around to fuss with the turkey, though for a few seconds I honestly couldn't see it very clearly. "You got somewhere to stay?"

"We have a hotel," Bill said.

"Got plenty of room here. But whatever you like."

They did end up staying. They brought in their things, and I set them up in the spare bedrooms, and I gave Mom Grace's bottle to feed her. She had one of the pink hats on already. When Travis came in, he looked surprised, but as soon as he saw I was okay, he kissed me, greeted his guests and asked what everybody wanted to drink.

We ate Thanksgiving dinner in the dining room

around the big table that had been delivered the week before, with my mom and brother and his wife and Haley and her parents and brother and my fiancé and my daughter, with the dogs sitting in the doorway hoping Travis would let them in, which he was not going to do.

The cardboard palm tree and battery lights were still on the walls from last winter's storm.

We got married the next March, in Council Bluffs, Iowa, so it would be legal and give us more protection for Grace. It was just a civil ceremony at the court-house. We had the reception and the big party at Nowhere. Mom and Bill and Sarah came out for that too.

They're still not always okay with it. They still think it's a little weird, I know. But they get better all the time. This summer, in fact, Mom is coming out for two months. Bill and I are trying to sort out where she's going to live because she can't be on her own at all now.

I would keep her here, but probably she is going to have to go into a home. Bill and I both agreed, though, it'd be best for Mom to be in Nebraska because nothing makes her happy quite like seeing Grace.

Grace is three now. I swear it was just yesterday I was sitting in the apartment above the barn while her mom told me she was pregnant, but it's been three years. We're looking at preschool for the fall. Haley has a list of places she says are okay academically and from a standpoint of not telling our daughter her dads are going to hell.

I actually wish I could keep Grace home longer. It all went by so fast.

The sex room, so you know, is in storage. We still play, but not as much because honestly I'm tired most of the time. I'm not ashamed, and it's not as if becoming a dad erased my kink, but right now with her so little, it changes things around. My focus has shifted, for the moment.

And even with a lock on the door, it's not something I think it's right for her to see. I'm not embarrassed about the way I like my sex, but I also know there is no way in hell I am explaining the sex bench to my kid until she's fifteen. Or eighteen. Maybe twenty-five.

She's in the other room right now, calling to me. I can hear Ez and Zeke outside going crazy over a rabbit they have cornered behind a shed, but Grace is louder. She wants to show me a picture, she says, of her home.

She's been into this lately. She doesn't say her house. She says her *home*. And when she draws the picture, it's always the same. She draws a big box house with a triangle roof, and she puts some brown and white squiggles off to the side which, she has told me, are the sheeps and the horsies and the cows. In the sky above the animals, she draws another box with a flag on top of it, with a person who is a head, four legs and lots of blonde hair. This is Mommy, who is off at school to teach people.

On the other side of the house there are three other people. Two more blobs, one with brown hair and one with yellow and gray. The blobs have four legs too, but the inside top ones reach over to hold up the round little egg with black hair and a wide red smile. In front of them are two black circles.

"This is my home, Daddy Roe," she says to me. "This is my house and my cows and my horsies. This is my sheeps. This is my mommy and her school. And this is me, and this is my daddies. My Daddy Roe and my Daddy Travis, and my doggies, and this is my home."

I crouch in front of her and I nod, and I say, because this is the way the game goes, "Where's my home, Gracie?"

She opens her arms and smiles like the sun and says, "Right here, Daddy!" as she pulls me in tight against her heart.

About the Author

Heidi Cullinan has always loved a good love story, provided it has a happy ending. She enjoys writing across many genres but loves above all to write happy, romantic endings for LGBT characters because there just aren't enough of those stories out there. When Heidi isn't writing, she enjoys cooking, reading, knitting, listening to music, and watching television with her husband and daughter. Heidi is a vocal advocate for LGBT rights and is proud to be from the first Midwestern state with full marriage equality. Find out more about Heidi, including her social networks, at www.heidicullinan.com.

Carry the Ocean

Book 1 of the Roosevelt series

Normal is just a setting on the dryer.

High school graduate Jeremey Samson is looking forward to burying his head under the covers and sleeping until it's time to leave for college. Then a tornado named Emmet Washington enters his life. The double major in math and computer science is handsome, forward, wicked smart, interested in dating Jeremey—and he's autistic.

But Jeremey doesn't judge him for that. He's too busy judging himself, as are his parents, who don't believe in things like clinical depression. When his untreated illness reaches a critical breaking point, Emmet is the white knight who rescues him and brings him along as a roommate to The Roosevelt, a quirky new assisted living facility nearby.

As Jeremey finds his feet at The Roosevelt, Emmet slowly begins to believe he can be loved for the man he is behind the autism. But before he can trust enough to fall head over heels, he must trust his own conviction that friendship is a healing force, and love can overcome any obstacle.

Warning: Contains characters obsessed with trains and counting, positive representations of autism and mental illness, a very dark moment, and Elwood Blues.

Check Heidi's website for buy links from multiple vendors.
www.heidicullinan.com/Carry_the_Ocean

Special Delivery

Book 1 of the Special Delivery series

When your deepest, darkest fantasy shows up, get on board.

Sam Keller knows he'll never find the excitement he craves in Middleton, Iowa—not while he's busting his ass in nursing school and paying rent by slaving away in a pharmacy stockroom. Then Sam meets Mitch Tedsoe, an independent, long-haul trucker who makes a delivery to a shop across the alley.

Innocent flirting quickly leads to a fling, and when Mitch offers to take him on a road trip west, Sam jumps at the chance for adventure. Mitch is sexy, funny and friendly, but once they embark on their journey, something changes. One minute he's the star of Sam's every x-rated fantasy, the next he's almost too much a perfect gentleman. And when they hit the Las Vegas city limit, Sam has a name to pin on Mitch's malady: Randy.

For better or for worse, Sam grapples with the meaning of friendship, letting go, growing up—even the meaning of love—because no matter how far he travels, eventually all roads lead home.

Warning: This story contains trucker fantasies, threesomes and kinky consensual sex.

Check Heidi's website for buy links from multiple vendors.
www.heidicullinan.com/books/special-delivery

Learn about the rest of the Special Delivery series here.
www.heidicullinan.com/taxonomy/term/12

Dirty Laundry

The course of true love doesn't always run clean. But sometimes getting dirty is half the fun.

Entomology grad student Adam Ellery meets Denver Rogers, a muscle-bound hunk of sexy, when Denver effortlessly dispatches the drunken frat boys harassing Adam at the Tucker Springs laundromat. Thanking him turns into flirting, and then, much to Adam's delight, hot sex over the laundry table.

Though Denver's job as a bouncer at a gay bar means he gets his pick of geek-sexy college twinks, he can't get Adam out of his head. Adam seems to need the same rough play Denver does, and it's damn hard to say no to such a perfect fit.

Trouble is, Adam isn't just shy: he has obsessive compulsive disorder and clinical anxiety, conditions which have ruined past relationships. And while Denver might be able to bench-press a pile of grad students, he comes from a history of abuse and is terrified of getting his GED. Neither Denver nor Adam want to face their dirty laundry, but to stay together, they're going to have to come clean.

This title is part of the Tucker Springs universe.

Check Heidi's website for buy links from multiple vendors.
www.heidicullinan.com/books/dirty-laundry

Other Titles by Heidi Cullinan

Look for free in-series shorts, excerpts, multi-platform buy links and more at Heidi's website (www.heidicullinan.com).

Standalone Titles

A Private Gentleman
Family Man (with Marie Sexton)
Dance With Me
Hero
Miles and the Magic Flute
The Devil Will Do
Clockwork Heart (coming soon)

Love Lessons

Love Lessons
Fever Pitch
Lonely Hearts (coming soon)

Minnesota Christmas

Let it Snow
Sleigh Ride
Winter Wonderland (coming soon)

Special Delivery

Special Delivery
Double Blind
Tough Love

The Roosevelt

Carry the Ocean (coming soon)

Tucker Springs

Second Hand (with Marie Sexton)
Dirty Laundry